Dear Reader,

I adore hot heroes. And I think Blake Landon definitely qualifies. His dedication to his country, his service and his friends are almost as sexy as his rock-hard body and gorgeous smile. He's perfect for Alexia, especially since he forces her to do the one thing she believes in so strongly for others, but avoids for herself—healing her past.

Alexia is a strong woman who follows her heart and believes in grabbing life with both hands. But can she let herself fall in love with a guy who breaks the two absolute rules she's set for her love life? He's military, and he's not only similar to her estranged father...he's her father's protégé.

I loved writing this story and bringing two such powerful, strong-willed characters together and watching them rescue each other. I hope you enjoy their journey, too.

And if you're on the web, I hope you'll stop by and visit. I'll be sharing Blake's breakfast recipe on my website, and insider peeks into this story and others. Stop by my website at www.TawnyWeber.com or find me on Facebook.

Happy reading!

Tawny Weber

A SEAL's Seduction

Tawny Weber

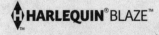

Recycling programs
for this product may
not exist in your area.

ISBN-13: 978-0-373-79742-4

A SEAL'S SEDUCTION

Copyright © 2013 by Tawny Weber

HARLEQUIN®
™ www.Harlequin.com

Printed in U.S.A.

ABOUT THE AUTHOR

Tawny Weber has been writing sassy, sexy romances for Harlequin Blaze since her first book hit the shelves in 2007. A fan of Johnny Depp, cupcakes and color coordinating, Tawny spends a lot of her time shopping for cute shoes, scrapbooking and hanging out on Facebook. Come by and visit her on the web at www.tawnyweber.com.

Books by Tawny Weber

HARLEQUIN BLAZE

To get the inside scoop on Harlequin Blaze and its talented writers, be sure to check out blazeauthors.com.

Other titles by this author available in ebook format.
Don't miss any of our special offers. Write to us at the following address for information on our newest releases.

Harlequin Reader Service
U.S.: 3010 Walden Ave., P.O. Box 1325, Buffalo, NY 14269
Canadian: P.O. Box 609, Fort Erie, Ont. L2A 5X3

Thank you to all of the men and women
who serve their country.
You are amazing heroes.

1

And they who for their country die shall fill an honored grave, for glory lights the soldier's tomb, and beauty weeps the brave...

—Joseph Drake

A LOUD BLAST FILLED the air as seven guns exploded in succession. Once, twice, thrice. Twenty-one shots. Faces implacable, the honor guard shouldered their guns and stood as tall and rigid as the oaks lining the cemetery.

The echoing silence broke when the bugler sounded taps. Lieutenant Blake Landon stood at attention, his eyes narrowed against the bright morning sun. The chaplain's words of honor, bravery and sacrifice rolled over him like the gentle breeze, teasing, hinting but not really making an impact.

There was no mention of Phil's sense of humor, of how he always carried a rubber snake on missions to break the tension. That he'd hit a McDonald's the minute they were stateside for a bagful of French fries. The chaplain didn't know that before jumping from a plane, Phil always kissed his mother's picture, then rubbed a rabbit foot. He wouldn't mention Phil's love for the beach. It didn't matter how godforsaken hot their assignment might have been, the minute he was off duty, he'd hit the beach—sun, surf and girls in bikinis. He'd often said those were his reward for getting shot at on a regular basis.

But that wasn't the Phil they were honoring right now.

Here, at Arlington National Cemetery, Lieutenant Phil Hawkins was a soldier. Here, the sacred tradition of honoring the noble warrior focused on service, dedication and sacrifice to country.

The entire SEAL platoon in attendance, Blake stood shoulder to shoulder with his team. His squadmates. The men he served with, fought with, trained with. Prepared to offer up the ultimate sacrifice for their country.

Later tonight, they'd all celebrate Phil, the man. Their squadmate, buddy, friend. The Joker.

He clenched his jaw, his eyes glancing off the flag-draped casket, then shifting to the distant trees again when the captain began the ritual of folding the red, white and blue material. As the chaplain offered his final words of comfort, the captain gently placed the folded flag into Mrs. Hawkins's hands.

Blake's focus locked on that triangle of fabric and didn't waver as the funeral finished. The people around him moved, shifted, left. He didn't. He couldn't.

They'd gone through BUDS training together. He, Phil and Cade. All cocky as hell, all determined to push their limits, to be superheroes. The Three Amigos, the rest of the team had called them. Inseparable.

Now permanently separated.

A large, beefy man joined him, scattering his thoughts. Grateful for the distraction, Blake directed his attention to the admiral. His hair as white and gleaming as his uniform, the older man topped Blake's own six feet by at least two inches.

"Lieutenant," Admiral Pierce greeted quietly. "I know this is a hard loss for you and your team. You have my sympathies."

"Thank you, sir," Blake said, his words stiff as he watched Phil's mom softly smooth her fingers over the folded flag, as if running her fingers over her son's cheek. Blake cringed when she lost it, her slender shoulders shaking as she sobbed into the triangle.

Desperate for distance, he ripped his gaze away. He looked at the trees. Oaks, mighty and strong, stood tall. Symbolic, probably. But he was having trouble finding solace.

"It never gets easier," the admiral said.

"Should it?" Blake asked, looking at the older man. His superior. His trainer. His mentor.

"No." The admiral glanced over at the trees. He sighed, then looked at Blake again. "No. But it's something you'll revisit. One way or another. Make sure you don't let it get in your way."

Just like that? Blake wanted to protest. To call bullshit on it being that easy to simply push the loss of his comrade, his friend, aside. But years of training, the respect he had for the man who'd recruited him to the SEALs, eliminated that thought almost before it formed. Instead, he inclined his head to indicate he'd handle it.

Clearly expecting exactly that, the admiral nodded. Then he cast an assessing glance around the graveside.

"Lieutenant Commander," the admiral called, his words carrying over the gentle grasses and soft murmur of the milling crowd.

Cade Sullivan, Blake's team commander and the third amigo, subtly came to attention. With a quiet word and a brush of his hand over Mrs. Hawkins's shoulder, he turned and strode across the lawn.

"Sir?"

"I'm assigning your men leave."

Blake and Cade exchanged looks. All it took was two seconds, a slight furrow of the brow and a shift of their shoulders to know both men were in perfect accord. They didn't want to go on leave.

"Sir?"

"Two weeks R&R, effective immediately."

For the second time since joining the navy—and both in the space of the last few minutes—Blake wanted to protest an order. He didn't want time off. He needed distraction. Work. A mission. Preferably one that included blowing up large buildings and letting loose vast amounts of ammo.

Fury was like a storm, brewing and stewing inside him.

It needed an outlet. The shooting range would work. Or the base gym.

As if reading his thoughts, the admiral inclined his head, offered a stern look and added, "You've just finished a tense mission, and lost one of your own. I hope you have places off base to stay, as I'll be leaving word at the gate that you're on inactive duty until September seventeenth."

For a second, Cade's usual charming facade cracked, the same anger Blake was dealing with showing in the other man's vivid green eyes. In an instant, it disappeared, and his smile—the one that lulled friend and foe alike into thinking he was a nice guy—flashed.

"Looks like it's time for a trip home. My father will be thrilled. Thank you, sir. I'm sure the team will be excited about the R&R."

You had to admire Cade's talent for lying. The man had a way with sincerity that, when added to that smile, was pure gold. At least it was if you weren't the one he was conning. The truth was, the team was going to be pissed, Cade hated visiting home and his father hated having him there. Yet the guy still smiled as if he'd just been pinned with the Congressional Medal of Honor.

That's why Phil had always called Cade Slick. Blake was Boy Scout. By the book, a goody-goody, his whole life was focused on being prepared. On being the best SEAL he could be. And Phil? He'd been the Joker. The last thing he'd said before that bomb had blown him in two? Knock knock.

Knock knock.

Jaw clenched, Blake glared at the sleek black lines of the casket.

Cade excused himself to inform the other men of their spiffy little vacation, leaving Blake and the admiral standing alone. The rest of the mourners were dispersing, civilians leaning against each other, shoulders low as they made their way across the lawn.

"Landon?" the admiral prodded. As if there was any option. Cade, like the admiral, was Blake's superior. He'd accepted the order, so it was a done deal.

"I'm sure I can find something to do," he said quietly. Not go home. He was less welcome in the trailer park he'd been raised in than Cade was at his big fancy mansion.

The guys were meeting later at JR's, the local bar and dance club Phil had favored. After that, Blake would go back to California. Drive up the coast, check out Alcatraz, the Golden Gate. Anything.

"I'll see you on the fifteenth."

Blake frowned. "I thought we were ordered off base until the seventeenth."

Had he misunderstood? Hell, it was only two days, but he'd take them.

"My retirement party. I expect you there. You can meet my daughter." With that, a stern smile and a clap to the shoulder that would have put a lesser man a foot into the ground, the admiral strode off.

Leaving Blake to contemplate those last words.

Meet the admiral's daughter?

Shit.

Hot. Hot. *Hot.*

There were a lot of things to be grateful for in life. Good friends. A healthy body. Chocolate-covered caramel.

All good.

But not nearly as good as the sight of a gorgeous, mostly undressed man. The kind of man who made a woman very aware of all her girlie parts.

The one striding along the water's edge was that kind of guy, Alexia Pierce's girlie parts assured her. Gorgeous, built and, since he seemed oblivious to the women he left panting in his wake, as humble as he was hot.

Tall, she'd bet his body lined up perfectly with her five-ten frame. Long legs ate up the sand as he strode toward the ocean, his deliciously broad shoulders straight, his flat belly framed by a tapered waist. He had that sleek, muscled look that said he could kick some ass, but didn't have the bodybuilder bulk that screamed mirror-whore.

Dark hair, a little too short for her taste, had just a hint of curl. She wrapped her finger around one of her own ringlets, figuring a guy who fought the wave would have a little sympathy when humid days made her look like a demented poodle. She couldn't see his eyes from this distance, but he had those dark, intense brows that made guys look ferociously sexy. Either blessed genetics or the summer sun had washed his body with a pale golden hue.

She wondered if he was just as golden beneath those summer-blue swim trunks. Was it too much to hope a big wave would help out in giving her a peek?

C'mon, waves.

The guy was a potent combination, guaranteed to make a strong, independent woman whimper with desire.

At least, in her own mind.

As she mentally whimpered, Alexia shaded her eyes against the bright arcs of sunlight reflecting off the Pacific and interfering with her view of the gorgeous specimen of manhood as he dived into the ocean.

She actually envied the water as it slid over that rock-hard body.

"Want a towel?"

"Hmm?" she murmured, absently taking the soft fabric that was handed to her. Frowning, she glanced at the red beach towel, then at her brother. "What's this for?"

"To wipe your chin."

"Goof." She laughed, tossing the towel back at him before sitting back on her beach chair, her toes digging into the warm sand. "That's sweat from the sun. I'm not used to it being this warm the second week of September."

Or, admittedly, to seeing a man sexy enough to make her sit up and drool.

"Right. It's the heat." Michael was a master at sarcasm, his words as dry as the sand beneath their feet. "Aren't you in a relationship?"

Even as Alexia waved that question away with a flick of her wrist, she yanked her gaze from the water. She didn't know why. Even if she were in a relationship, looking wasn't cheating. And at this point, she and Edward were just colleagues who'd dated a few times. Friends—without benefits. Buddies, even.

"Not so much in a relationship as considering one. Dancing around it, maybe," she admitted. More like trying to justify pushing herself into taking a handful of dates and a solid friendship and making them something more.

Something bigger. Of course, she'd been trying to talk her-self into it for three months now. If there was one thing Alexia was good at, it was talking. "I don't know what we are, to be honest."

Michael tilted his red sunglasses down to peer at her. His eyes were the same dark, depthless brown as her own, but he was blessed with thick lashes while she was stuck relying on volumizing mascara. It'd be so easy to hate him for that. "You moved across the country for a guy. That says relationship to me."

Alexia lifted her bottle of water and sipped, her eyes sliding back to the ocean. All she could see of the swim-mer was the occasional elbow. Why did that turn her on so much more than the idea of seeing all of Edward, naked?

Which was the problem in a nutshell. She liked every-thing about Edward. The man was brilliant, one of the foremost scientists specializing in psychoacoustics. She'd studied under him for two years when he was in New York, before he'd moved to California to take over the Science Institute. They had a lot in common, enjoyed each other's company and always had a ton to talk about.

The only problem was, she wasn't sexually attracted to him. And she couldn't imagine a relationship without sex. Without heat. Excitement and orgasms and spontaneous wall-banging releases. Those were as high on her relation-ship list as honesty and communication.

"I moved across the country for a once-in-a-lifetime job. That says career to me," she said as she dug her bottle back into the sand. "This position is off-the-charts exciting. I'll be doing in-depth research into correcting and enhancing sexual recovery for abuse victims by means of subliminal messaging, neurolinguistic programming and brain-wave technology. And get to be the face of the Reclaiming Yourself project. I'll meet with investors, promote the project and make a difference in how it's perceived by the press."

"You're an acoustical physicist with a minor in psychology. How does that translate into PR shill?"

Alexia grimaced at her brother's irritated tone.

"Show a little more enthusiasm, why don't you," she said, swiping her towel at him. "It got me back to California, so you should be grateful. Investors want to talk to someone directly involved who is working on the project. I'm better at the social stuff than Edward is, and since the project focuses more on female sexuality, it's better to have a woman front and center."

"In other words, Dr. Darling isn't as good at talking sex as you are?"

Alexia grinned, but as the words sank in, her smile dimmed. Yeah. Edward was great at the science of sex. But talking about it? Doing it? She wasn't so sure.

"I'm just giving you a bad time. I really am excited that you're back home," Michael said, patting her shoulder. He gave her a cheeky look. "With you here, publicly talking sex all the time, the heat's going to be off me with the parents. So thank Dr. Darling for me, 'kay?"

Alexia's smile disappeared completely.

"They're going to have a fit, aren't they?" she murmured.

"Yep."

By the time she'd started third grade, Alexia had known three things. One, that she was much, much smarter than the average bear. Two, that she didn't quite fit in anywhere—not with kids her age, not with the agenda her parents lined up for her and not with what her child psychologist had deemed *society's norms*. And three, that her father would never love her. After a few years of exploiting the first while trying to hide the second, she'd finally realized that there was nothing she could do about the third. At thirteen, with a slew of academic awards, a couple of skipped grades and a social calendar filled with normal, acceptable, shoot-me-now-I'm-going-crazy boring activities, she'd done a tight one-eighty.

She'd stopped socializing and started failing classes. She'd turned to fatty food and sugar for comfort. She'd explored more ways to numb herself than she liked to remember. And to this day, she wasn't sure if her father had noticed any of that.

But he had noticed when, at sixteen, she'd been picked up by the base MPs, drunk and half-naked with an ensign thirteen years her senior. That'd been the second turning point in her short life. Her father's fury hadn't mattered. His blustering and disgust had barely dented her hangover. Seeing that, the admiral had proceeded to show her once and for all where she got her brains. In an ice-cold voice, he'd promised that the next time she stepped out of line, she'd be out of his house and no longer a part of the family. She'd shrugged, saying that she didn't care. He'd nodded, as if he'd expected exactly that response, before adding he'd then send Michael to boarding school overseas.

Michael. The one person who loved Alexia. Who accepted and celebrated her. Who she'd be cut off from until he was eighteen, if their father had any say in it.

Yep. The admiral was a scary man.

"Don't stress about it," Michael said quietly, clearly tracking her trip down memory lane. "Mom's thrilled you're back and Dad will come around eventually. They might not like what you're talking about, but the prestige of seeing you on TV, hearing you're at the big fancy billionaire parties like any good socialite will bring them around."

"Sure, as long as they ignore the part about me publicly talking sex." Alexia sighed. As much as she wanted to be tough and emotionless when it came to their parents, a part of her still craved—with the desperation of a small child—that approval. But she couldn't—wouldn't—change who she was to get it.

"You could almost feel sorry for them." Michael laughed. "We're not exactly their idea of poster children, huh? To make it easier on them, when I go to Sunday brunch, I pretend to be straight. Not an easy thing for the headliner of Sassy's Fancy, an all-male revue. Last month I mentioned my photo shoot for Calvin Klein and you'd have thought I tried to jump the waiter, the way Dad choked and Mom sputtered."

"Maybe they'll focus more on the fact that this research project will potentially help abuse victims overcome their fears than the sex part of things," Alexia mused. When her brother looked at her as if she'd jumped right over naive into delusional, she wrinkled her nose.

"So enough about how proud we make the parents," Michael said with a dismissive wave to both the topic and the low-level guilt Alexia was starting to feel. "What's the real deal with you and Dr. Darling?"

"Edward's last name is Darshwin," she corrected for the zillionth time, following his lead and sitting up to reach for the sunscreen. Unlike many redheads, Alexia didn't have a problem tanning. She did, however, turn into one giant freckle after too much sunshine. "And I don't know what the deal is, really. He's a sweetie. Smart, cute and really big on communication. A guy who likes to talk feelings. What's better than that?"

"A guy who makes you feel things worth talking about," Michael ventured quietly.

Yeah. She sighed. That.

"When did you get so smart?" Alexia slanted him a

look. Spread out on a bright turquoise beach towel, he looked too pretty, and honestly too vain, to offer up such deep thoughts. Sleek and toned, he was a man who made his living by looking good.

"Babe, just because I'm not a superbrainiac like you doesn't mean I'm not a pretty sharp cookie."

Wasn't that the truth.

Joy, as warm as a big squishy hug, filled her. Alexia could have turned down the job offer that'd brought her back to San Diego. But between her dream job and a chance to live close to her brother again, she hadn't been able to resist. They'd grown up as military brats, and the only steady thing in their lives had been each other. And while she didn't look for a lot of steadiness these days, she needed love. Needed to feel important. Special. If only to one person—and even if that person was her brother.

As if taunting her with Michael's words, her gaze sought out the gorgeous specimen of manhood again. Now, *that* was a guy who'd make a girl feel things worth talking about. She let the sight of his body, cutting strong and sure through the ocean waves, soothe her. Relax away the tension and worries.

Then he stepped out of the water.

And a whole new kind of tension seeped into her body.

At the same time, all thoughts, and most of her brain function, vanished. Every cell of her being was focused, like a laser, on his body.

His gorgeous body.

Sleek muscles, from the top of his sexy head to his well-shaped feet. The man was a work of art. Not in the bodybuilder-obsessed way, but pure streamlined power.

Him, she was sexually attracted to. Him, she could easily see herself begging for.

"You know, I might have questioned your judgment and

hairstyle over the years," Michael said quietly. "But I've never faulted your eyesight. That is one fine-looking man."

"He's okay," she downplayed as if her body wasn't melting just looking at him.

"Okay? Just okay?" Michael's voice rose in indignation, as if she'd just insulted gorgeous men everywhere. "What'd New York do to you? You say you're not in a relationship, but your butt's still planted on this towel. Why aren't you going for it?"

"Because, as you pointed out, I'm in a relationship."

"*Considering* a relationship."

"Which means I should *finish* considering before I do anything crazy," she retorted. "Like hit on some stranger just because he's gorgeous."

"Gorgeous is the best reason to hit," Michael mused. Then he gave her an arch look. "Of course, he might not be your type."

"I don't think he's yours," she said with a laugh, eyeing the sexy swimmer. A man who exuded that much sexual energy, who made her wonder how many hours it'd take to try her top ten favorite *Kama Sutra* positions, gay? That'd be a crime against women everywhere.

"Let's find out, shall we?" Michael suggested as the man walked toward them, either because his stuff was up the beach past where they sat or maybe in response to intense do-me signals Alexia was mentally sending.

"Michael," she hissed, suddenly wishing she were on a plane back to New York. Or buried in the sand. Either would be better than what she knew was coming. "Don't you dare."

"Did you say dare?" Michael's grin shifted to one hundred degrees of wicked.

"Michael." Jackknifing upright, Alexia made a grab for her brother's arm. And growled when she missed.

"Oh, hey, excuse me," he called as he slid gracefully to his feet. "Do you have a second?"

Gorgeous slowed, walking toward them. His eyes—yes, just as fabulous as the rest of him—bypassed Michael to lock on to Alexia.

His gaze was like being bathed in a deliciously sensual bath. The dark blue depths were warm, luxurious and bone-meltingly wonderful.

Alexia swore she felt the world shift. Or maybe it was just the sand beneath her butt as her brother hurried forward to offer his hand.

"I'm Michael," he said, his smile big and bright as he gestured her way. "That's my sister, Alexia."

"Blake," the man introduced quietly, his voice carrying just a hint of the South.

"I was wondering if you wanted to join me, us, for a drink?" Michael reached into the cooler and pulled out a bottle of water, offering it. "It'd be a great favor. You can help settle an argument between my sister and I."

BLAKE GLANCED AT PRETTY BOY, and the proffered water, then at the sexy beach siren lounging at his feet. She looked like a parting gift from summer, as hot as the season itself. All red hair and gold skin, she made his mouth water.

Any other time, he'd have made a move to join her. But instead of offering healing, solace, the last two weeks had simply hammered home his grief. Made it worse. He'd hung out at Cade's apartment for a while. Only back a couple of days from a visit home, Cade had been lousy company. Silent, morose and distant, wallowing in the bitch of a mood that always went with dealing with his family. So Blake had escaped to the beach.

The sun hadn't helped. Neither had the surf. And he was

sure talking to strangers was just as pointless. *Just make an excuse and go,* he told himself.

"What argument?" he heard himself asking instead.

"Alexia thinks a hot date is dinner and a movie," the guy told him, tilting his bright red sunglasses down his nose to offer a comical eye roll. "Boring, right? Me, I think a club and dancing is the way to go. What's your take?"

The bottle of water halfway to his mouth, Blake paused to stare.

Was the guy hitting on him?

Tempted to laugh, Blake offered the redhead a baffled look. Her answering smile was like a ray of sunshine, reaching out to pull him out of a dark hole he hadn't even realized he'd been hiding in.

"Both," Blake said. "Dinner and dancing. I'm traditional that way."

"Ah." The guy's smile didn't shift, his attitude didn't change. But his nod made it clear he'd got the message that he wasn't Blake's type. "Then I guess it's a draw."

"You'll have to excuse Michael," the redhead said. "He's a nothing-ventured, nothing-gained kind of guy."

"Can't fault him for that."

"You're sweet," she decided softly, her smile flashing bright. At first glance, her features weren't traditionally beautiful. They were too striking, too bold. Eyes almost too large for her face were direct under a slash of dark brows. Her jaw was strong, her lips full with an obvious underbite that spelled all kinds of sexy to Blake's suddenly wide-awake libido.

A red-rose tattoo on her shoulder twined down her biceps, twisting and circling. Her body, hot enough to make a man grateful for summer, was stunning. Packaged in a tiny purple swimsuit that hugged and highlighted curves, he suddenly wished like hell he'd met her another time.

One when he could lavish on her every bit of attention she deserved.

Blake was the kind of guy who'd built his career on doing the right thing. Who lived his life by the rules. He not only followed the book, but double-checked it to ensure the rules he was following were exactly as written.

Anal?

It worked for him.

At least, it had.

The image of Phil flashed through Blake's mind, the last thing he'd seen from his buddy was his big, cheesy grin just before the shrapnel had pierced his helmet.

Phil had followed the rules.

The entire team had, to the letter.

And they'd still lost their teammate.

Overwhelmed by the memory, Blake turned to stare toward the ocean, trying to find peace again. The water wasn't giving any up, though. Of its own volition, his gaze returned to the stunning redhead.

She didn't look like the kind who followed rules.

Maybe that's what he needed right now.

His eyes traveled over the smooth golden skin of her bare belly, noting the tiny strings tying her bikini bottoms to her slender hips. His body stirred. Blood pumped. For the first time in two weeks, he felt alive.

He'd come here to heal, though.

And as much as losing himself in a body as lush and welcoming as Alexia's appealed, he knew better. A smart man fighting demons avoided addictive substances. Alcohol, drugs, gambling. Gorgeous, sexy women. Anything that let a man numb himself to the memories.

Blake's body screamed a number of ugly epithets at him. Ten years in the navy meant it had a ton to choose from. Still, he'd put his body through worse than denying it a gorgeous woman. He'd get over it.

"Thanks," he finally said, splitting his smile between the brother and sister. "But I've got to go."

Before he could change his mind, he lifted the water bottle in acknowledgment, and strode away. And regretted every step.

2

"EDWARD, I'VE THOUGHT about it a lot," Alexia said, her tone low in an attempt to keep their conversation private from the rest of the diners. After her talk with Michael on the beach that afternoon, she'd realized she had to deal with the issue before she started work the following week. "I value our friendship, it's really important to me. But I don't think we should risk it by trying to turn it into more."

After uttering those totally uncomfortable words, Alexia held her breath and waited for Edward's response. Sounds suddenly amplified, forks against plates, the rushing servers' feet against the tile floor, even the sound of the still-warm tortilla chips sliding into salsa.

The smile not shifting on his handsome face, Edward blotted his lips with his napkin, then took a sip of his water. Buying time to sort his reaction, Alexia realized with a wince.

"I'm sure we'll be fine. Nerves are natural before taking a big step in a relationship. Don't let it worry you."

No. Anticipation was natural. Excitement was. And sure, nerves if they were along the lines of *will he like seeing me naked* and *is he open to kinky positions*. But this stomach-churning, feet-twitching-to-run, little-voice-screaming-nooooo feeling? This wasn't normal.

What did she have to say to get through? She really didn't want to hurt him.

But after her reaction earlier that morning to hot, sexy and gorgeous on the beach, as she still thought of the hottie named Blake, there was no way she could settle for a sexless relationship. Spark, desire, passion, they were too important. It'd been all she could do not to chase the guy down the beach, throw herself at his feet and beg him to let her make up for her brother's odd behavior by licking her way up his body.

Heck, she'd stayed so turned on and sexually charged thinking about him, she'd come twice in the shower preparing for this dinner. Clearly her subconscious was sending her a strong message that she and Edward weren't meant to be a couple.

But he wasn't listening to her subconscious. Or her words, for that matter. What did that say about their wavelength? Edward had a habit of believing that if he ignored something he didn't like, it'd eventually go away. Having tried that often enough, and still having the parents to prove it didn't work, Alexia could empathize.

"Sweetie, we have a great time together," Edward said brightly, dismissing her concerns with a wave of his fork. His blond hair glinted in the colorful piñata-shaped lights and his perfect teeth flashed. "We're great together. We're on the same wavelength, totally in tune. Our interests, our goals, our values, they all click. That's what counts, right?"

Alexia forced her lips to curve in agreement. Because he was right. They were in tune and did have a great time. But that wasn't enough.

"That's all important," she said, pushing her barely tasted enchiladas aside to reach across the table and take his hand. "But those are things that make for a strong friendship. Not a…"

She couldn't do it. Alexia wanted to pound her head on the table a few times to try to shake the words loose, but didn't figure it'd do much good. So she took a deep sip of her pomegranate margarita—her third—instead. How was she supposed to say that she had absolutely zip sexual interest in him? She specialized in the art of subliminally messaging the center of the brain that controlled sexual response. She was about to start a job that required her to be front and center, publicly talking about how to heal and stimulate sexual responses. How could she work with test subjects and expect people who'd had sexual trauma to trust her to help them if she couldn't even talk about her own sexual needs?

"Look," Edward said, twining his fingers with hers. "I know what you're worried about. That mythical spark isn't blazing between us. You think there should be some energy, some physical manifestation of attraction."

It was all she could do not to throw her hands in the air and say *duh.*

"And you don't?" She'd worked enough in the field of sexual health to know there were men who couldn't perform. Others whose libidos were so low, they had no interest in sex. But she wouldn't have thought that Edward fit that category. He was a geek, sure. And a little socially awkward sometimes. But if he had issues, he wouldn't hide them. He'd self-diagnose and dive into treatment, using himself as a test subject.

"Our species was made to experience sexual connections," she said, shifting the discussion into scientific mode instead of personal, and instantly relaxing. "You know the statistics as well as I do. The odds of a romantic relationship lasting without sex are slim."

"Alexia, relationships based on sexual heat don't last. They flare hot and intense, then burn out just as fast." Edward leaned forward, his words as sincere as the fervent look on his face. "Better to base a relationship on more solid, long-lasting emotions. Like friendship and similar interests. We share the same values, the same goals in life. That matters more than a few paltry orgasms."

Well, sure. If they were paltry, she could see his point. Who needed that? Alexia thought, dumbfounded.

"We're scientists who specialize in sexual health," he continued. "Layering the physical elements into our relationship won't be an issue. And when we do, it'll be done in a well-thought-out, practical and measured way. Just as it should be between two intelligent scientists focused on the long term."

Well… Wasn't *that* sexy.

Alexia drained her margarita, the bitter tang of the pomegranate matching the taste on her tongue. Was that how she came across? As the kind of woman who would settle for measured practicality? In bed? There was only one thing she wanted to be measuring in bed.

Edward must have sensed her disquiet, because he shook his head, as if to stop her from saying anything.

"Think about it," he said, giving her fingers one last squeeze before trading them for his fork again. "In the meantime, don't worry about us. Get settled in your apartment, enjoy the weekend. Maybe reacquaint yourself with some of your old haunts. That'd be fun, right? Don't you have a family event this weekend?"

"My father's retirement party," she acknowledged with an inward cringe. How fun was that going to be? The only thing that might appeal more was finding a gynecologist with a hook for a hand. Alexia signaled the waiter for another margarita.

"Just let it go for now. Let your subconscious work it through. I'll wait awhile before I bring it up again." He looked so sincere, so sweet, that it actively hurt to have to set him straight. But she wasn't going to change her mind, and the sooner he accepted that, the sooner they could reestablish their friendship on its original terms. Alexia sighed, then, not seeing any choice, opened her mouth to tell him that she'd made up her mind already.

As if reading her intention, he hurried to say, "In the meantime, did I tell you about the latest round of crackpot threats the institute is getting?"

"The bitter women's brigade is protesting sex again?" she asked, giving in and graciously letting him change the subject. That was part of the art of communication. Read the signals in order to know when to talk and when to let things go until a better time. Between his sidestepping the issue, refusing to listen and stiff-shouldered body language, she might as well give up. For now.

He nodded. "Oh, we hear from the women's brigade about once a week. But this was a new one. A European gentleman wanted to offer us a grant to study anger and aggression."

"There have been a number of studies in that area," Alexia said, smiling her thanks to the waiter as he swapped her empty glass for a full one.

"Not with the focus of using subliminal messaging and brain-wave manipulation to incite anger."

"Incite? Isn't five o'clock on the 405 freeway enough to do that?"

After a brow-furrowed second, Edward quirked a smile, then shook his head. "Apparently not. This gentleman offered a huge sum of money. Enough that I was actually tempted, if not for the fact that we're already so committed to the current project that it'd hurt our reputation to pull out at this point."

Well, *goody* for future funding and the need to keep up one's reputation. She hadn't signed on for anger management, and didn't like the idea that Edward and the institute's focus could be bought. Alexia gripped her fork so tight it left a dent in her fingers, but managed to smother the anger before she made a nasty remark. Dating, friendship and the rest aside, Edward was still her boss. Calling him a greedy weasel was probably a bad idea.

But she'd taken the position at the institute because she wanted to help people. Because she knew the power sexual satisfaction could offer and truly believed that everyone deserved a chance at that kind of pleasure. Not to make money for whoever had the deepest pockets.

Her mind flashed back to hot, sexy and gorgeous on the beach that afternoon. As she let herself focus on the image of his butt, so tight and solid beneath those wet swim trunks, the red edges of anger faded from her vision. Now, *that* was the kind of guy who inspired fantasies and made a woman very, very aware that she was female. But for women with issues, whether from conditioning or abuse, that delight was out of reach.

Too bad she hadn't gotten a chance to see if the reality of hot, sexy and gorgeous was as delicious as the fantasy. She could have called it work incentive.

Or just mind-blowingly awesome sex.

AN HOUR AND A HALF later, Alexia paid the cab and stepped onto the shell-encrusted sidewalk in front of JR's. The club-slash-bar fronted a long stretch of beach, both lit up like carnival attractions.

She wasn't sure why she was here. She definitely didn't need another drink. But she didn't want to go home, either.

And the idea of spending any more time with Edward, pretending that everything was peachy keen, was enough to make her scream. She wanted to dance. To relax in a crowd of strangers. And JR's was the only bar she knew well enough to feel safe. A regular hangout of the navy locals, it wasn't that it didn't get rowdy or wild. But it had three major advantages. One, it was a familiar place so she knew what she'd get when she walked through the door. Two, she was there to dance, and if anyone tried to push for more, her get-out-of-trouble-free card, aka the mention of her father's name, would cut them off at the knee. And three, she'd never get involved with a military man. Ever. She'd had enough of the military growing up to know that a sailor's first priority was to his very dangerous, often secretive career. And while she respected that, she had no interest in being background noise in someone's life.

Still, walking into the club was like stepping face-first into chaos. Noise, so loud the music had to be felt instead of heard, pounded through her. Heat from the crowd of bodies swirled with an ambitious air conditioner. Lights flashed, strobed and glowed, depending on which way she turned her head.

Maybe she should have just gone home.

But she'd have gone crazy there, with only her thoughts and guilt for company. Michael was on a date, and three days back wasn't enough time for her to have made any new friendships. So she was on her own.

And she needed action. Movement. Something to shake off the sexual tension that'd been driving at her all afternoon. Since hunting down the sexy guy from the beach wasn't an option, she'd figured she'd do the next best thing to release body tension. *Dance.*

About to head for the flashing lights of the dance floor

and kick up the heels of her favorite Manolos, a man at the bar caught her attention.

Blake?

The hot, sexy and gorgeous from the beach?

A slow, wicked smile curved her lips at the sight.

He was just as appealing dry and clothed as he'd been wet and half-naked. In jeans and a simple T-shirt that did wonders for his broad shoulders, he looked like a guy who just wanted a drink and some alone-time. Too bad for him, though, since a blonde barracuda was tiptoeing her red talons up his chest. Was that his type? Blatant, busty and ballsy? He grabbed the blonde's hand on its downward sweep, shaking his head. She didn't back off. Alexia bit her lip to keep from laughing at the range of emotions chasing across his face. Irritation, confusion and just a hint of amusement. Poor guy, he probably hadn't realized this was a navy bar. Which meant pushy, desperate women all focused on one thing. Catching themselves a sailor boy.

He looked as if he needed saving.

Sliding and pressing her way through the crowd of bodies, she made a path to the bar. The music was quieter here, but the cacophony of voices made up for it. She was about five feet away when Blake's gaze found her. Delight flared in those blue depths, making her girl parts feel oh-so-happy. Happy enough that she hesitated. Getting all hot and wet over a stranger wasn't a bad thing. But it wasn't where she was at in her life right now, either. Despite what she'd told Michael, she had feelings for Edward. Ones that deserved to be explored. She couldn't explore feelings for one guy while another was tickling her girlie parts. It just wasn't right.

But could she leave Blake there at the mercy of the red-taloned barracuda?

As if sensing her struggle, Blake gave her a wide-eyed

look of desperation. *Hurry up,* he mouthed. Alexia's lips twitched, but her feet started moving again.

She bypassed the blonde and positioned herself behind Blake. Heavily made-up eyes glanced her way, dismissing her with a flick of false lashes.

It was going to take stronger measures, Alexia realized. Warning her girlie parts not to get too excited, she moved in close, draping her arm over the broad muscles of Blake's shoulders. He was like steel. Solid, strong, sleek. Her mouth watered. To give it something to do before she actually drooled, she leaned forward to brush a friendly kiss over his cheek. He smelled like the ocean. Clean, salty, intoxicating.

"He's with me," she said, giving the blonde a go-away tilt of her head.

"He's not wearing a ring."

Alexia's expression didn't change. All she did was curve her hand over Blake's shoulder. Possession. Then she leaned her body closer to his. Whether he knew what she was doing or he was preparing to use her for a shield, he wrapped his own arm around her waist, pulling her tight to his side.

Desire sent her body into a tailspin at his touch. Warm tingles swirled, heating her nipples to pebbled warmth before trickling down to her belly. Because he was sitting on the bar stool and she was standing, his head was level with her shoulder. All it would take was for him to turn his head and his lips could brush her nipples.

Alexia had to force her breath to steady, her vision to clear. She couldn't do anything about the damp heat between her thighs as her girlie parts did a happy dance, though.

"Like I said," Alexia repeated as soon as she knew her voice was steady, "he's with me."

Proving that brains and bleach weren't mutually exclusive, the barracuda hissed through a smile clenched so tight her jaw had to ache, then shrugged.

"Fine. You two have fun," she said. Flicking a challenging look at Alexia, she leaned against Blake, pressing so tight her silicone squished out the sides of her tank top. She sank both hands into the sides of his neck, pulled his head down and slapped a slurpy wet kiss on his shocked mouth.

"Just in case you change your mind," the blonde said when she released him.

Grinding her teeth, Alexia almost reached over Blake's shoulder and smacked the smile off the blonde's face. Whether it was just her nature, or a by-product of the red hair, anger was an emotion she visited daily. But jealousy was brand-new to her. Trying to tamp down the green-eyed gnawing fury in her belly, she decided it wasn't one she liked.

Still, her fingers curled into a fist and her eyes narrowed as she sized up the other woman. At five-ten and dedicated to her gym membership, Alexia was pretty sure she could take her.

"I guess I'll join my friends now," the blonde said, looking a little afraid.

Subliminal messaging at its best.

Realizing that she still had her hand fisted, Alexia took a deep, calming breath and relaxed her fingers. Then, because she really needed the rest of her body to relax, too, she shifted away from Blake. Touching him was anything but calming. It took another deep breath before she had enough control to put on a friendly expression and walk around to face him.

"Thanks," he muttered, shaking his head as he watched Blondie sashay away. Like if he took his eyes off her before she'd reached a safe distance, she might ricochet back and plaster herself all over his body. "She wasn't interested in hearing no."

"It's a hard word for some people to accept," Alexia agreed with a grimace, thinking of her dinner date. "I spent most of my upbringing trying to get people to listen when I said no. Or yes. Or anything, actually."

She tried to laugh away her discomfort at oversharing. Communication was important. But it was a two-way street, not a one-way emotional dump. Blake didn't look uncomfortable, though. More…curious.

"You don't seem like a wimp to me," he said after a long contemplation.

"Well, aren't you the sweet talker," she said, both amused and relieved. Not that she figured on tossing him over her shoulder and carrying him off to have her wicked way with his body or anything—mostly because he was too heavy to carry. But she'd hate to think that she was on par with the barracuda when it came to scaring guys off.

"Sweet talk is a game, isn't it?" he said. Then he shrugged. "I don't play games."

Ooh. Intriguing. If his sexy body hadn't already caught her interest, the idea of finding out if he was for real—or if that statement was simply a game in itself—would have hooked her for sure.

"That must be tough, being a nongame kind of guy in an arena like this." She twirled her fingers, indicating the lights, the bar, the bodies. "In here, like in life, almost everyone is playing a game of some kind."

He looked around the bar, his expression blank. Just a little lost. As if he wasn't sure how he'd got there. Alexia's heart clenched. He was so wounded. She wanted to wrap her arms around him and pull him close. Let him rest his head on her breasts while she combed her fingers through his dark hair.

Her nipples tightened as if preparing for just that.

What'd happened that he felt so much pain? Maybe if she got him talking, he'd open up. Let it out so he could start healing.

Radiating damp heat and fresh off the dance floor, a guy tried to get past her to order a drink. Alexia wedged herself between Blake's body and the bar stool. Now it wasn't the music throbbing through her body. It was desire, hot, intense and needy. Nothing wrong with that. She was a red-blooded woman with a healthy appreciation for her sexuality. Didn't mean she was going to act on it.

Maybe.

BLAKE WATCHED the sexy redhead closely, mulling over her comment. He didn't like to think of himself as a game player. But she was right. Everyone probably did play games in one way or another. Hell, the military called them war games. A test, pitting man against man. Even man against himself. The endurance and strength training, weren't those games of sorts?

And the mental gyrations he'd been playing before the blonde had tried to dig her lethal claws into him. It'd be a game, pure and simple, trying to convince himself that he'd exaggerated Alexia's impact in his mind. That she wasn't as sexy, as gorgeous, as appealing as he remembered.

But now that she was standing in front of him again? She had the same impact as an unexpected fist to the gut. Shocking, intense and demanding an instant response.

Her personality was as bubbly as her looks. Fiery curls, golden skin and molten dark eyes topped a body that made a man want to get on his knees to offer thanks…among other things.

The memory of her body, each and every delicious curve of it highlighted by tiny scraps of purple fabric, was etched in his mind. So he didn't begrudge the loose fit of her dress, high at the neck but leaving her shoulders bare, the turquoise pleats barely skimming the tips of her breasts before draping to midthigh. Her legs were bare. Yards of silky golden leg stretched between the bottom of her dress and skyscraper heels.

"So," she said after a long pause, her voice a little breathless. He wondered where her mental trip had taken her. And what kind of games it'd included. And if he'd been there. Maybe naked.

"So," she said again, clearing her throat then giving him a bright, friendly but not flirty smile. "What brings you to a club like this? It doesn't seem like your kind of place."

"Why not?"

"This is navyland," she said, waving her hand around the room. "Soldiers and sailors, this is their hangout. Most guys avoid it unless they're stationed at Coronado."

Blake frowned into his beer before taking a drink.

"You don't think I belong here?"

He didn't know how to take that. He'd joined the navy the day after he'd graduated high school, and had found his home. His place in the world. With the SEALs, he'd found family. He'd never wanted to be anything else.

"Oh, I don't know. You've got the body and the, well, energy, to be a sailor boy," she said, her tone still teasing as she gave him a slow once-over. Her big brown eyes slid from his face and down his body. Proving he was alive and doing damn well, his body stirred in reaction. Hardened.

"But?" he prodded when her eyes stayed a little too long on his jeans. A few more seconds and she was going to be seeing a whole different terrain down there.

"But you don't have that bravado I usually associate with soldiers," she said a little breathlessly, looking into his eyes again.

"Bravado, hmm? Is that a requirement, something they issue along with the uniform?" He grinned. Maybe Cade was right. Maybe he was burned out. He liked the sound of that better than wallowing in grief. Whatever it was, he kinda liked that Alexia didn't know he was a sailor. With her, he wasn't Lieutenant Landon, decorated Navy SEAL, radioman, linguist and teammate. He wasn't a finely honed weapon, a highly trained warrior. He wasn't a military paycheck, or a score to be notched.

He was just a man.

That was so damn appealing.

"I think bravado is intrinsic," she decided. "It either fits, or it doesn't. But a uniform probably helps."

"And you like the uniform?" Figured. Most women did. Most women didn't even look past it. Plenty of guys didn't care. Whatever bait worked, they reeled 'em in. Blake was pickier than that, though. And oddly deflated to think that Alexia wasn't.

The bartender delivered a fresh drink and took the empty. Blake nodded his thanks and lifted the bottle, ready to wash some of the bitterness off his tongue.

"I'm not a fan, actually."

Thirst forgotten, Blake slowly lowered his beer. *Not a fan? Seriously?*

Seeing his shock, she grinned. "Don't get me wrong. I appreciate our servicemen and women. They are amazing. But when it comes to relationships, I'd rather steer clear."

"Relationships?" He pulled a face. Women always used that word. What it meant was sex with a soldier—and let's face it, SEALs did everything, including sex, better. Or a golden ticket to a soldier's paycheck and benefits without the day-to-day work of being a wife.

Blake realized that this was probably the first time since he'd enlisted that he'd had a flirt going on with a woman who was only focused on him. Not the SEAL thrill. Yeah, this just-being-a-man thing was wildly appealing. He didn't consider it a lie not to tell her he was navy. She'd made the assumption, after all. He was just letting her go with it.

"Yes, relationships." She laughed, bringing him back to the conversation. "I'm a fan of the concept."

How much of a fan? A groupie type? A desperately chase-after-it type? Blake frowned. Was she in one? Would she be here if she was? You never knew with women. He debated asking. The problem was, once that discussion door was open, it went both ways.

"But most women here," she continued, waving her hand again to encompass the loud club. "They're all about the goal, not the relationship."

"What's the goal?"

"Fishing. They're here to fish for sailors," she said, shifting closer so she didn't have to shout the words. Close enough that her body heat wrapped around him, her scent filled his head with the image of sun, surf and sex. "Some, like Blondie, are catch and release. Others are looking for a keeper."

"That's awfully cynical," he observed, laughing even though her words echoed his own thoughts. "Aren't you women supposed to stick together? You know, group bathroom trip, the girl code, the secret sisterhood?"

Dark eyes dancing, Alexia leaned closer. Blake almost held his breath so as not to be tempted by her scent. Coconut, spices, just a hint of something floral and purely female. Then he remembered he was a solider. A navy SEAL, for crying out loud. He was brave enough to deal with sexy.

"Oh, believe me, if she was a friend I'd be distracting you while she slid that hook into your mouth," she assured him with a laugh. "But tonight, you look like you could use someone on your side."

Nonplussed, Blake stared. And saw the sympathy in her eyes. As if she'd seen into his soul and wanted to soothe the pain there.

God, he was a mess. When had he lost it? Blake had been captured by the enemy once. They'd been furious with his implacable refusal to show emotion or reveal information. But tonight all it took was three beers, and a sexy redhead could read his secrets?

He figured he had three options. Say goodbye and walk away before she delved any deeper. Open up and share the confused emotions tangled in his gut. Or distract her.

But he never gave up, and he wasn't into sharing. So option three was it.

"Which category do you fall into?" he asked, giving in to the need that'd been gnawing at him since that afternoon and reaching out to touch her. Just the ends of her hair, like silken heat between the tips of his fingers.

"I don't think I can be categorized," she murmured. "It's too easy to be dismissed once a label's been posted, isn't it?"

Beautiful, sexy and smart? She might as well be wearing a sign proclaiming her dangerous territory.

A woman this perceptive was better to hustle along as quickly as possible. When a man's defenses were down, it was smart to keep the threats to a minimum. Out of the corner of his eye, he noticed Cade and a group of SEALs saunter into the club. Now that his teammates were here, she'd find out he was navy soon enough. Still, Blake figured it was better to hurry her along before he was tempted to do something stupid.

"Everyone can be categorized. The only question is, are you in the catch-and-release group?" he asked quietly.

"Or are you looking for a keeper? And if it's not the uniform that gets your attention, what's a guy got to show? His bank statement?"

There. That should piss her off. Blake sipped his beer with only a little regret that he was driving away what could have been the most incredible encounter of his life.

3

HER TEMPER WAS A WORK OF ART. First Alexia's eyes flashed dark fire. Then they narrowed as if she was contemplating where she wanted to punch him. Blake didn't bother to steel his core. He deserved the hit, and he'd take it full on. After all, that'd been a cheap shot.

"C'mon," she said, tilting her head toward the exit.

Not sure he'd heard her right, Blake frowned in confusion as she wriggled between him, the bar stool and the three guys blocking her way.

Blake's groan was lost in the noise of the club. With her in heels, her lips were within kissing distance of his. Her breasts, full and soft under that flowy dress, skimmed, just barely, his chest. He knew it wasn't deliberate. He'd been hit on enough to tell. But it was the sexiest move he'd ever felt.

"C'mon," she said again, this time waving her fingers in a *let's-go* gesture.

Still baffled, but with the rational side of his brain sputtering due to the feel of her breasts sliding like white heat against his chest, Blake followed. His eyes on the sway of her hips as he headed for the door, he didn't lose sight of her even as he took a short side trip to where his friends were waiting.

"I'm outta here," he said, tilting his head toward Alexia's back.

Cade followed his gesture, gave an impressed arch of his brows and a thumbs-up.

"Glad to see you're using your time wisely," he said with a grin before heading toward the heart of the club noise to party it up in his usual style.

Blake didn't worry about blowing off his buddy. And given that the lieutenant commander was wearing a T-shirt that claimed Navy SEALs Don't Make Deals, he didn't feel bad about not making introductions, either.

He did, briefly, think joining Cade and the rest of the guys might be smarter than following Alexia outside. Those guys were trained to have his back. But some missions just had to be done solo.

Stepping out the club doors into the warm night air, he gave himself a second to adjust to the lack of noise. Nothing better than silence, with a little ocean music, to set a chewing-out to.

Alexia stood toward the end of the building, where the wooden walkway curved toward the ocean. Hands fisted at her hips, she sucked in a breath through gritted teeth, her eyes flashing fire.

"You sure you want to tear me down for the insult privately?" he asked before she could say anything. He flashed his most charming smile to indicate that he knew he had it coming and wouldn't protest her angry retaliation. "Don't you want witnesses?"

"Actually, I figured you needed a little air. You know, to clear the testosterone idiocy out of your head before you said anything even stupider." Then, the fury clearing from her eyes, she laughed.

Laughed? Where had the anger gone? She was like mercury, changing so fast he could barely keep up.

Damned if that wasn't tempting. She was sexy and fun, with so much energy he felt alive again. He wasn't sure if he wanted to, though. Maybe it'd be smarter to turn heel and go back into the club. Or, he fingered the keys in his pocket, hop in his truck and drive away.

"Not that you don't deserve a little teardown," she continued with a shrug that highlighted well-toned shoulders and the golden glow she'd got at the beach that morning. "But I figure a guy smart enough to know he's made an asinine comment is smart enough to not make it without a reason."

Huh? Blake rocked back on his heels, trying to figure that one out.

"I got too close, right?" she guessed. "You're upset about something and here I come, a total stranger, poking and prodding like I have the right to peek into your privacy. So you slapped me back. That's natural."

"Are you for real?"

"Why? Because I didn't have a hissy fit?" She tilted her head to one side, her curls bouncing around her face. "Do you think women are that easily categorized?"

"I think this is where I got in trouble," Blake mused. He still wasn't buying the no-games line. But he was intrigued enough to want to see if she could change his mind. "Want to walk?"

She gave him a narrow look, then glanced at the tiny boardwalk leading to the beach. Smart women didn't wander off with strangers, so he didn't take offense. But since there was a party going on along the beach, it looked like a wedding or something, she must have decided there were enough numbers for safety.

She gave him a considering look. As if she was debating something beyond safety. For a second she looked as though she might think he had the potential to haul an ax out of his back pocket. Then she lifted her chin and offered a bright smile.

"Sure."

As soon as they reached the point where the wooden slats gave way to silken sand, Alexia stood on one foot to remove her shoe, then switched to the other. Not sure when he'd become a gentleman, Blake held her hand to help her balance. Her fingers were dainty. Slender and fragile. Warm. Strong.

The kind of fingers that would feel incredible skimming over his naked flesh. Tugging his zipper down and gripping his hardening erection. Stroking, guiding.

Hell. As soon as she was barefoot, he not only grabbed his hand back, he put a safe couple feet between them. The woman was potent.

"You're not taking yours off?" she asked.

"Nope." To end the discussion, he strode onto the beach, his tennis shoes sinking, sand filtering into his socks. Didn't matter. He had the feeling he'd do better to keep every article of clothing intact.

Although he didn't have Cade's track record and fancy-faced looks, he'd had his fair share of women hitting on him. Hitting back always depended on three things.

Timing. Was he fresh off a mission and in need of shedding some pent-up energy, or about to embark on a mission, which would provide him with an inarguable exit strategy?

Spark. A lot of guys he'd served with banged anything that moved. For the notch, for the cheap thrill, to stroke their ego. Whatever. Blake didn't want notches, thrills or strokes when he got naked with a woman. What he did want was spark. Heat. Something wild and intense, like the rest of his life.

But the most important return-hit factor was the commitment perspective. Years of SEAL training had sharpened his instincts to a razor's edge, and years of avoiding commitment had honed his ability to discern a woman's intentions—even if she didn't realize them herself.

Timing and spark didn't mean jack if the woman's perspective was skewed toward long term.

The redhead smiled. A slow, wicked curve of her lips. It didn't matter that the look wasn't aimed at him. Blake's muscles still bunched, his senses sprang to full alert and his dick hardened. Yeah. There was plenty of spark. It was the timing, and the scary depths of her perception, that worried him.

"I've missed the beach," Alexia said after a few minutes of silent strolling along the water's edge.

"Where've you been?"

"New York." She gave him a saucy look, her eyes sparkling in the moonlight. "Can't you tell from my accent?"

Before training for the SEALs, Blake had served as a cryptologic technician. In civilian terms, a linguist. He spoke fluent Spanish, Russian, Arabic and Persian. And once in a while, pretty decent English.

"I meet a lot of people from a lot of places," he told her. "Most are easy to place by their accents. You don't have one, though."

"Seriously? I don't have any accent?"

He grinned at her affronted tone.

"I'm an expert," he assured her. "Take it from me, you're accent free."

Then, maybe because he was starting to relax for the first time since watching Phil's helmet blown to smithereens, he decided to show off a little.

"Bet you moved around a lot as a kid. Not just the U.S. Your tones are too rounded to be purely American. Europe. Maybe Asia?"

She stood rock still, music from the party ahead filling the air with a Motown beat, her hands fisted on her hips, and gave him a narrow-eyed look. "Did Michael track you down and say something this afternoon?"

Blake laughed. There wasn't a whole lot to do for entertainment on a ship in the middle of the ocean, so he'd built a rep guessing where the guys were from. *Name that accent in ten words or less,* Phil had called it.

His laughter faded. The memory didn't hurt as much, though. Maybe it was the dark. Or the company.

"Your brother didn't spill any secrets," he assured her. "I told you, I'm good at accents."

"You really are clever." She laughed, the sound as alluring and mysterious as the ocean itself. "I'll bet it's a handy skill. Does your job involve languages?"

"Yep." But he didn't want to talk about his job. He wanted to escape it right now. He watched her dip her feet in the surf, kicking up droplets and catching them in her fingers. What'd it feel like to be that free? That comfortable with yourself, with life. "What about you? You a psychologist or something?"

"Like I said. Clever," she complimented as they reached the edges of the party. People milled about, dancing in the light of tiki torches, diving fully clothed—and in a couple cases totally unclothed—into the night surf. "I have a minor in psychology, actually. But I don't practice."

"What do you do?"

"Until recently, I worked at a private New York lab as an acoustical physicist."

"Seriously?" he asked, throwing her word back at her. A science geek? With a minor in psychology? Blake fingered his keys again, figuring he could make it up the beach to his truck in about six seconds flat.

"Yes, seriously," she chided with a laugh. "I specialize in psychoacoustics."

What was that? Crazy talk?

He shifted on the balls of his feet, gauging the sand's inertia effect on his escape.

"And psychoacoustics is…?" he asked tentatively.

"The technical definition is the study of sound perception, measuring the psychological and physiological response to sounds."

"So you do research?"

"Research, development," she agreed with a shrug before giving him an arch look. "My current research is focused on correcting and enhancing sexual health through subliminal messaging, neurolinguistic programming and brain-wave technology."

Intrigued, a little confused and, since she'd mentioned sex, totally open to being turned on, Blake settled his weight again, raised one brow and invited, "Tell me more."

From the amused look she gave him, it was clear she knew which part he wanted to hear more about.

"If done right, subliminal messaging offers an opportunity to bypass the brain's critical factor and speak directly with the subconscious. This is where the changes happen. Not just changes like smoking cessation or breaking a sugar addiction. But true physical changes. When trauma or conditioning are too strong for someone to overcome, the best way to make changes is on a subconscious level. This could be a powerful tool in helping abuse victims overcome blocks, in making inroads to libido dysfunction, healing emotional confidence."

Between the animation in her voice and the way she was practically glowing with excitement, it was clear this was a woman who got passionate about her work. He gave her a questioning look. "So you're talking about using sound to do the work of a psychologist?"

"Sure. It's a little deeper than that, and should actually be done in concert with psychotherapy instead of replacing it, but you have the general idea of it right."

Blake was all for a little mood music while doing the deed, but this was wild. Then again, he was getting pretty turned on just listening to her talk, that husky voice so passionate and excited—even if it was about her job rather than something more personal, like his body.

"How'd you go from acoustical physics to sexual health?" he wondered.

"While getting my psych degree, I interned at a clinic that helped abuse victims. It was heartbreaking," she said quietly, staring out at the water. "Years, lifetimes were impacted by a single event, and no matter how much these people wanted to overcome that, or how much we tried to help them, there were things that the mind just wouldn't let them get past."

Blake didn't say anything. He couldn't. His own mind was taking its oft-hourly trip back to the mission, to his last sight of Phil. She was right. Some things, they just didn't go away.

"I'm boring you, aren't I?" she asked, giving him a rueful look, the moonlight glistening off her downturned lips.

"Hell, no. I'm fascinated. Besides, I like a woman who gets this excited about sex," Blake said with a wicked grin.

"Done right, sex is the ultimate excitement," she said, her voice as sultry as the night itself.

"And done wrong?"

She smiled, slow and wide. Her look was filled with empathy, a sort of deep sympathetic understanding that told him this was a woman who cared. Not just about her job. But about people, about helping. About making things better.

And he'd thought she was scary when she was just perceptive.

Trying to regain control over the needs raging through his libido, Blake focused on the scenery. A few yards from the water's edge, a crop of boulders marked the end of the beach. Up the dune, a large white tent sheltered the bulk of the wedding party, music pouring a soft wave of romance down toward the surf.

"Want to sit?" he asked, gesturing toward the bench-like rocks. "Or are you ready to head back?"

She nibbled her bottom lip, making him want to beg her to let him do it for her instead. The full flesh glistened, damp, in the tiny white lights twinkling around the tent. Since grabbing her would pretty much guarantee an end to the evening, he forced himself to be patient while she decided.

"We can sit for a few minutes," she finally said.

Waiting for her to settle herself on the rock, watching her carefully arrange her shoes next to her, he wondered what she'd been thinking. What had been the deciding factor between staying or going?

"So you love your job," he said, leaning his hip against the rock so he was half facing her, half facing the water. "What else are you passionate about?"

Her fingers toyed with the tall grasses growing between the stone, the blades black in the moonlight. It was hard to tell since he couldn't see her eyes, but she suddenly seemed sad. As if he'd rapped his knuckles on a healing bruise. Since he felt like one giant bruise himself, he could sympathize.

Before he could change the subject, she glanced up, her lashes a feathery frame to the intense look in her eyes.

"You know, I don't think I've been passionate about anything except work for a long time. I learned pretty young that my passionate exuberance for certain things in life was a problem. So I pulled it in. Focused it. First on school, then on my career."

Her words were matter-of-fact. But so sad, he felt like a self-pitying fool for settling into a pit of grief the way he had. For hiding instead of facing life the way Alexia did.

He should ask about her past. Find out what had hurt her, how she'd overcome it. Give her the comfort of getting it off her chest.

But the idea of that made his gut ache like no amount of enemy fire or threat of torture could. Feelings, emotions, opening up. They all seemed passive. He was a man of action. So he went with comfort-option number two. His body gave a silent woohoo.

He lifted her hand, amazed at its softness. Long, slender fingers trembled once. He watched as she took a quick breath, stilled her hand and lifted her chin. In a rare move, his body reacted without his say-so, hardening.

"All work can't be good, even when it's work you enjoy," he said. "You should share that passion. Spread it around to other things. You know, maybe a hobby."

"Hobbies are good," she agreed softly, the look on her face both amused and patient. As if he was a cute little kid who entertained her. Not quite the image he'd been going for.

"But I think there are other things I'd rather be passionate about," she said, her words almost lost in the pounding of the surf.

Or was that the pounding of his heart?

She was in trouble. Knee-deep, sinking-fast, scream-for-help-before-it's-too-late trouble.

Alexia knew all the signs.

Her heart was racing, even as her feet twitched, warning to run.

Anticipation curled, tight and low in her belly. Somewhere between desire and terror, it waited. Hope and fear entwined, making it impossible to know which to root for.

Her mind screamed warning, but her body wanted him, badly. Her nipples tightened and her thighs melted in anticipation. It was all she could do not to close the space between them, lean into that rock-hard body and trace her tongue over the hint of stubble along his jaw. She'd bet he tasted yummy.

Catching herself just before she fanned her hand in front of her face to try to chill, Alexia desperately grabbed control, reeling it tight.

It was time to make an excuse and leave. She had a very narrow window—maybe five minutes, tops—before she did something really, really stupid. And she'd spent a lot of years weaning stupid behavior from her repertoire.

She was proud of that. Even as a sneaky part of her brain whispered that she'd been good for so long, she deserved a little bad. Just a little, now and then.

Mostly now.

Then Blake stepped closer. Her eyes widened. Her pulse tripped over itself before racing off so fast it made her light-headed.

"I know it's too soon," he murmured, his words as dark and deep as the night sky, "but I have to taste you."

Alexia's mental gymnastics melted away, right along with her resistance. Desire swirled down into her belly in a slow, sinuous slide.

Then his lips brushed over hers and she didn't care about stupid, resistance or the fact that they were on a public beach.

His breath was warm. His lips soft. The fingertips he traced over her shoulder a gentle whisper. It was sweetness personified. She felt like a fairy-tale princess being kissed for the first time by her prince.

And he was delicious.

Mouthwatering, heart-stopping, panty-creaming delicious. And clearly, he had no problem going after what he wanted, she realized as he slid the tips of his fingers over the bare skin of her shoulder. Alexia shivered at the contrast of his hard fingertips against her skin. Her breath caught as his hand shifted, sliding lower, hinting at, but not actually caressing, the upper swell of her breast.

Her heart pounded so hard against her throat, she was surprised it didn't jump right out into his hand.

She wanted him. As she'd never wanted another man in her life. Years, she'd behaved. She'd carefully considered her actions, making sure she didn't hurt others. She'd poured herself into her career, into making sure her life was one she was proud of.

She had a man who wanted her in his life. A nice, sweet man who she could talk through the night with and never run out of things to say.

But she wanted more.

She wanted a man who'd keep her up all night screaming with pleasure. Who'd drive her wild, who'd send her body to sexual places she'd never even dreamed of. She wanted orgasms. Lots and lots of orgasms.

Even if it was only for one night.

And that, she realized, was the key. One night of crazy. One night of delicious, empowered, indulge-her-every-desire sex with a man who made her melt.

One night would be incredible.

One night would be enough.

"This is crazy," she murmured against his lips.

"Yeah," he agreed, his tongue sliding over her lower lip before he nipped the tender flesh. When she gasped, he soothed it with a soft kiss. "But crazy feels damn good."

It did.

She wrapped her arms around his neck, leaned into the hard, solid wall of his muscled body and gave a low moan of delight. He felt really, really good.

Blake pulled back then, giving her an intense look. As if he was trying to see past her heart, into her soul. As if he knew all her secrets, her every desire.

Then he smiled. A slow, wicked curve of his lips. As if he'd just figured out how to make every one of those desires a reality.

Now, *that* was a scary proposition. Scarier still, she was pretty sure he could.

She wanted him. Wanted nothing more than to strip him naked and run her hands over every inch of his hard body. To touch, to taste. To feel. Oh, God, she wanted to feel him. To give herself tonight to feel, to enjoy. To live.

"Did you ever want something you knew you shouldn't have?" she asked, her words so soft they almost disappeared in the sound of the surf. She traced her fingertip over his lower lip, then sighed and met his eyes. "Something you knew you'd be better off not even considering, but were so tempted by?"

"No."

Figured. Alexia laughed helplessly, dropping her forehead to his shoulder and closing her eyes.

"But I know what it's like to want *someone* that bad," he said quietly, his voice so intense she had to raise her head to look at him.

He shifted, sliding his hands in a whisper-soft caress up her cheeks, then tunneling his fingers into her hair. Cupping her head just above her ears, he tilted it back just a little and stared deep into her eyes.

Alexia shivered. Her heart skipped, then tumbled over itself trying to catch up.

His gaze was hypnotic. Penetrating. The moonlight glowed, glancing off his cheekbones and giving him an otherworldly air. As if he was straight out of one of her fantasies, sent by the universe as a reward for her being such a good girl for so long. A chance to be bad again for just a tiny little bit of time, and then she could go back to being on her best behavior.

She wanted Blake, and this feeling between them. His hands skimmed through her hair, fingers tangling softly in her curls. This delicious, overwhelmingly intense feeling of excitement. Her body hummed, her senses went on hyperalert. It was as if each touch of his fingers was amplified, exciting her more than she'd ever been before. More than she'd even imagined.

"Shouldn't we talk about this?" she asked, desperately trying for sane and practical. "Make sure we know what we're doing?"

"Babe, I promise you, I know what I'm doing."

Whether to prove it, or to shut her up, he shifted again, his fingers strong, firm against the back of her head as he held her face up for his lips.

His tongue tangled with hers, demanding a response, pulling passion out of its worried hiding places and daring it to dance. Alexia's fingers dug into his shoulders as her mind gave up the fight to be rational and dived into the delights he offered. To hell with discussing it. Who needed a clear understanding of what the parameters of this exchange were when the communication between their bodies was coming through loud and clear.

Sexual nirvana, his body promised.

Hers couldn't respond with anything but *Let's rock.*

4

BLAKE SPENT A GREAT DEAL of his life under fire. He'd honed his body to be a strong, powerful weapon, ready to face down and beat any danger.

He was pretty sure he'd never felt so out of control as he did right now. It was as if Alexia was a sudden addiction he couldn't do without.

"You feel so good," she breathed, her hands gripping his shoulders, then sliding down the hard muscles to curve over the rock-hard roundness of his biceps. "So strong. Big."

"You ain't seen nothing yet," he said, his laughter a whisper of air over her throat.

"Then show me," she challenged. Using her nails, she scraped a soft line back up his arms and shoulders, then down his shoulder blades, pulling his body closer against hers.

He groaned in reaction, both to her move and her aggressive attitude. She was clearly a woman who knew what she wanted, and wasn't shy about getting it. Was there anything sexier? Still, they should probably go somewhere. Since he lived on base, and was currently banned, he'd been bunking at Cade's. So that was out. A hotel seemed tacky. Her place?

She leaned in, her breasts softly pressing into his chest as she placed tiny, nibbling kisses along his jaw. When she reached his ear and blew a soft gust of warm air, he groaned again.

He wasn't going to last till they found somewhere else. He had to have her. Here. Now.

Eyes narrowed, he peered up the beach. Their chances of being caught were slim. To narrow the odds even more, he swept her into his arms.

"Whoa," she exclaimed breathlessly, automatically wrapping her hands behind his neck for balance. He shifted her tighter against his chest and strode around the copse of boulders, far away from curious eyes.

"Better," he decided as the dark blanketed them, the rocks blocking the party, the lights and the people. He gently set her on a stone ledge, the height of it putting her breasts at mouth's reach. He stepped between her legs, nestling there. Exactly where he wanted to be. "Perfect."

Before she could comment, or worse, protest, he took her mouth again. She tasted sweet. Like sunshine and smiles and a hint of strawberries. Delicious. He was starving for more.

He rested his palms on her knees for a second, warming her skin before he caressed his way up the smooth, silky warmth of her thighs. He felt her shiver. Her breath caught. So damn sexy. He traced the edge of her dress, the fabric soft and smooth, but nowhere near as soft as her skin.

She was his escape. When he touched her, everything in his mind shut down. All the dark thoughts, the emptiness, they went away. It was as though the hollow desolation of the last month just disappeared. Instead, he had a single focus. Pleasure. Feeling it, giving it.

And keeping her totally focused on this passion between them, so she wouldn't think to slow it down. Because he was pretty sure if she stopped him, he'd make an embarrassed fool of himself and do something really crazy.

Like beg.

His tongue danced soft and slow over hers as he skimmed his hands down to her knees, then back up her thighs. He cupped the back of her thigh in one hand, shifting her so that her legs rested against his hips. With the very tips of his fingers he traced a gentle path along the edge of her panties, right there in the crease of her thigh. Hip bone to the top of her thigh, then back. A little deeper, a little closer to her core. Then back to her hip bones. His fingers slid down again, slipping under the slender elastic as they went. Teasing, loving how tight she felt as he wound her up, he stopped just short of her tempting flesh.

Her fingers dug into his arms, her thighs trembling at his touch. Her breathing intensified, and he could feel her heartbeat beneath his fingers, fast and furious.

He shifted his mouth over hers, taking the kiss deeper. Their tongues dueled, each fighting for control. She challenged him, stirred up a desperation he'd never felt before. The taste of her was beyond words. So delicious. So incredible.

Then she shifted. Her body beckoned, her warmth luring him closer. He needed more. He had to feel her. His fingers slid along the elastic of her panties again, this time hooking into the tiny lace band holding the sides together. He pulled.

She gasped as the fabric slid down her legs, then caught. Moving fast, again, needing to touch, to taste, he shifted so he pulled her panties away, then tucked the fabric into his back pocket. In less time than it took her to inhale, he was back. Right there between her thighs. Her warmth.

Delicious.

The movements had pushed the wildly patterned fabric of her dress higher, to the crease of her thighs. The moonlight shone on the hint of curls peeking from beneath. Beckoning. Tempting.

Blake didn't have the power—didn't want to find the strength—to resist temptation when it came in the form of Alexia. Starting at her knee again, he slid his index finger up the inside of her thigh. Wanting to see her reaction, he locked his gaze on hers. His fingers combed softly through curls that were gratifyingly damp, then skimmed the swollen bud nestled there.

Her gasp filled him with as much pleasure as touching her did. She squirmed a little, as if trying to intensify the pressure. Always glad to make a lady happy, he did just that. She gave a breathy moan, her hands now roaming his chest, scraping a delicate path of fire down his pecs and making him want to strip naked and see what she'd do next.

Her touch was perfect. Just the right blend of rough and delicate as her fingers scraped lower, along the flat planes of his belly. He sucked in his gut, wanting her to delve lower, to touch him the way he was touching her. Wanting to see how fast, how hard, they could go at each other.

Pulling his mouth from hers, he buried his face in the delicate curve of her throat, breathing deep her scent. It turned him on even more.

"You're delicious," he told her as he pinched her swollen clitoris softly. It was like triggering a switch. Her entire body stiffened, her breath coming in gasps now. She went up fast. He'd bet she was wild once she caught fire. Wild enough to take anything he had, to handle the intensity of his sexual appetite.

SHE WAS ON FIRE. Hot, intense and wet, Alexia gasped at the pleasure Blake's body offered. She let her suddenly too-heavy head rest against the rock as his fingers slid, first one, then two, deep into her core. Slid and swirled. Heightening and tightening.

It was as if he had her entire body, her entire being, in the palm of his hand. Literally. His to control. His to pleasure.

Oh, please, yes. More pleasure.

She pressed herself tighter against his hand, her hips undulating, circling, trying to take him in deeper. Her breath came in gasps, all of her being focused on his fingers. On the feelings he stirred. The scent of the ocean mixing with Blake's subtle cologne adding to the surreal, out-of-this-world feeling she had.

It turned her on even more.

The sound of people partying, just on the other side of the rocks, made her nerves sing, worry about one of them venturing this way adding a whole 'nother level of intensity to the feelings Blake's fingers were creating.

She'd never been an exhibitionist. She'd never been turned on by the idea of public kissing, let alone semi-public orgasms. But this was…

Oh, my God.

Her breath came faster as his fingers worked her.

Her heart raced, trying to keep up with the wild, intense feelings rioting through her body. She couldn't think, could barely breathe. Everything she had, everything she was, centered on Blake. His fingers, the pressure.

Oh, baby, the pressure.

Desperate for him to feel as good as he was making her feel, she skimmed her fingers, just the tips, along the hard, rounded muscles of his arms. His body was incredible. Masterful.

She wanted to touch him, to fan her hands all over the firm, sculpted planes of his body. But she couldn't find the energy to move. Not while he was doing such lovely things with his fingers. She was so focused on that, she barely noticed his other hand slide under her dress, up to her breasts, until he cupped one, squeezing tight.

"Oh, God," she moaned breathlessly, staring up at the stars overhead through blurry eyes.

His thumb brushed over her nipple. Sensation, sharp and enticing, shooting from her clitoris to her breast like lightning. With a quick flick, he unsnapped the front closure of her racer-back bra, the fabric breaking loose under her trapeze dress. The constrictive straps slid down her shoulders. Hating the trapped feeling, she quickly shrugged off the white satin, not caring where it fell.

She grasped his head with both hands, pulling his face to hers. She had only a brief glimpse of the flaring heat in his blue eyes before her mouth attacked his. Ate him up in big, gulping bites.

His fingers pinched, rubbed, swirled. Her nipples hardened, aching for more. As if hearing their pleas, he pressed harder, flicking his thumb back and forth, back and forth. Her body tightened. Her girlie parts wept with pleasure. His fingers moved faster between her thighs, plunging deeper into her core.

Then he pressed her aching bud tight with his thumb, his fingers—all of them—still tormenting.

The climax grabbed her so fast, she couldn't stop the cry of pleasure. Vividly aware that there were people nearby, she tried to stifle her screams, so instead they came out strangled gasps. Everything spun in circles. Her head, the stars, the hot delight low in her belly.

Before she could come back down, before her body was even through shuddering, he moved. She was vaguely aware of the sound of ripping foil as he readied himself.

Her thighs fell wide, as if begging to feel his hard power there, thrusting deep.

Instead, though, he grabbed her, lifting and turning at the same time so it was him bare against the rock.

She cried out in surprise, then in pleasure, as he pulled her close. Her body, still quaking from that lovely climax, wrapped around his.

His hands were so big, each one covered a cheek. He pulled her forward, gripping her flesh with strong fingers, positioning her. The velvet knob of his penis pressed, just there against her still-quivering flesh, as if begging for entry.

"Ready for some passion?" he asked, his words husky and low.

"Sure," she breathed, linking her fingers behind his neck and preparing for what she hoped was going to be a wild ride. "Because so far it's been pretty bland."

His laughter rang out, the sound making her ego feel almost as good as her body did with his pressed against it.

Then he slid, hard and deep, inside her.

She'd been wrong.

Nothing, ever, had felt this good.

It was as if her nerve endings all picked up and moved between her legs, every single sensation in her body connected to the feel of his cock driving in and out.

He moved slowly, with just a hint of undulation as he plunged. His hands gripped her butt, his strong fingers adding a whole new level of pleasure to the experience.

"You're going to come for me," he muttered, his words tight, low. Intense.

As if under his command, she instantly went over.

Alexia's body shook with the power of her climax. Her breath came in gasps, pleasure so tight, so intense, it bordered on pain. Her ears rang out, the surf disappearing so all she could hear was her own pounding heart.

As her body slowly settled back down to earth, she tried to catch her breath. Tried to reconnect with reality. Given that tiny trembling orgasmic aftershocks were still rocking through her, it wasn't easy.

All she could hear was his breathing, and the sound of her own heartbeat, loud and throbbing in time with his thrusts. Despite their semipublic love nest, she had a surreal sense of being outside the real world. As if this side of the rocks sheltered them in their own little bubble, away from real life. Away from repercussions or choices. Her head fell back, making way for his lips along her throat. For his kisses. His tongue.

It was as if he was flipping the switch from hot to blazing, bring her back to life, back to total awareness. Of the warm night air. The sound of the surf. The feel of his shoulders, so strong beneath her fingers. And his erection, still so hard and huge inside her.

"More?" she murmured.

"At least two more," he promised.

She gave a breathless laugh. No way. She didn't think she had two more orgasms in her. She had him in her, though, so she was ready to be proved wrong.

"Big talk," she teased, her fingers twining through the short hair at the back of his neck.

"Hold tight," he said, shifting his grip so his fingers were tighter on her butt. "Proof is on its way."

Then he leaned down, unerringly finding her pebbled nipple through the fabric of her dress and sucking hard. She shuddered, moaning over and over in time with his thrusts.

The tension wound again, tight and low as she gave herself over to the power he had over her body. Clearly he was a man who liked a challenge, and if he said two more orgasms, then dammit, she'd be reveling in two more mind-blowing orgasms.

He nipped, his teeth working her nipples through the wet silk. Alexia popped like a champagne cork, pleasure spewing from her in an explosion. Her nipple beaded, hard and aching beneath his lips. Her stomach constricted as heat curled lower, spinning tighter.

"That's one," he counted breathlessly.

And zero for him. As her body drifted back to earth, Alexia realized that he was calling all the shots. Not a bad thing, since those shots felt so damn good. But she wasn't the passive type, and she had a few shots of her own. She wanted him to go over. Wanted to drive him so crazy, he couldn't control himself. Wanted to feel him explode, to know that he felt as wild for her as she did for him.

But she couldn't use her hands because letting go of his shoulders meant she'd probably land on her butt in the sand. If she leaned forward to use her mouth, he might lose his grip, or worse, the perfect position he'd found that had his dick sliding against her clitoris with every thrust.

All she had were her hips, and those were in his hands. Still…

Calling on her thrice-weekly pilates training, she constricted her core muscles, her glutes flexing so she could grip him tight, like a fist, as he slid inside her.

He gasped. Groaned. His next thrust was hard and deep. Then he sucked in a breath and yanked himself back under control.

Oh, so he thought he could resist, did he? She gave a wicked grin. And clenched him again, this time swirling her hips against his.

The move sent yet another orgasm spiraling through her, her clitoris quivering, her breath rasping in and out.

That's all it took to send him over.

He thrust, hard, out of control. Intense, pounding pleasure poured through her as he gave a low moan, his body shaking as he poured out his climax.

Alexia's head dropped against his shoulder, her thighs trembling too hard, muscles too liquefied to keep them wrapped around him any longer. So she let them drop, her toes sinking into the soft sand. She felt as if she'd run a marathon while having a deep-tissue full-body massage and eating herself into a chocolate coma, all at the same time.

Pretty damn incredible.

Blake shifted, just a little, making the sand beneath her feet cave in a few inches. The sounds of music, of the partyers' voices, carried on the night air, dancing just above the surf.

Suddenly, awareness poked its sharp fingers through the fog of sexual delight. Made Alexia aware that she was practically naked, although her dress kept her modesty intact. That she'd just had three screaming orgasms with a virtual stranger, on a public beach, with a bevy of other strangers just yards away.

Holy cow, what had she been thinking?

Where had her good sense gone?

And why did she know, without a doubt, that given the chance, she'd do it all over again? What did that say about her? And, suddenly going all girlie, she cringed and wondered what Blake thought about her actions. Other than gratitude for one hell of a fine ride.

Cold, even though the temperature hadn't changed, she stepped out of his embrace. Unable to look at him, she rubbed her hands up and down her arms and made a show of looking around for her underwear.

"Well, I guess you showed me," she said, her words

as shaky as her laugh. She would have pushed her hands through her hair, but between his fingers earlier and the sea air, she knew she was probably already rivaling Bozo in volume. So she settled for twining her fingers together.

Alexia jumped when his hands closed on her upper arms. She automatically looked into his face, meeting his gaze. Warmed by the calm affection in his blue eyes, she felt a little of the tension drain away. Why was she ashamed? Healthy sex, between two consenting people? She gave a mental eye roll at the sudden, silly and totally not-her inhibitions that'd taken hold.

And wished like crazy that the eye roll was enough to make them go away.

Blake let go of one of her arms, reaching up and rubbing his thumb over her lips. A gentle caress quickly followed by an equally gentle kiss. When he pulled back, she sighed.

"I'd say we showed each other," he said quietly.

It wasn't a promise or declaration. It probably wasn't even meant to be a reassurance. But she felt as if it was both. A promise that he didn't think less of her and the reassurance that he'd stepped just as far outside his normal as she had.

"I guess we did." Her smile was about as big as her lips would stretch, but still not even close to how large and bright the bubble of joy inside her chest felt. "I suppose you should get back inside and meet that friend?"

She nibbled on her bottom lip, anxious to hear his response. He didn't make her wait long.

"Nah. We can go inside and have another drink if you'd like, though." He didn't sound excited. But he didn't let go of her, either, so she took his lack of enthusiasm to be for the drink, not the company.

Alexia took a deep breath. She'd told herself one night. And she'd already proven that she wasn't a chaste good girl who required a ring—or hell, even dinner—for a sex romp. So there was nothing to stop her from grabbing on to her *entire* night.

"Did you want to go back to my place?" she asked. "I just have to call a cab."

His lips shifted, a slow, sexy smile curving his mouth. The kind that lit up his eyes and made her want to hug him close because he was so damn cute.

"I've got my truck." He let go of her and reached into his pocket, handing over her panties. "You might want these, though. I held on to them so they wouldn't get all sandy."

"Aren't you the gentleman," she teased, gratefully taking the tiny scrap of silk.

"You know it. And I'd like to think the only abrasions you're going to have on your thighs are coming from my whiskers."

Alexia's breath caught. Her heart danced. And her body—which should be sexually satisfied enough to last for weeks—did a giddy little cheer.

"Then let's see how soon we can make that happen," she said, wriggling into her panties, then holding out her hand.

When he wrapped his fingers in hers, she began the mental chant *one night, one night, one night*.

One helluva night.

5

Everywhere Blake looked was desert. Weapons fired around him, shots flaring like fireworks, bright and loud. Their quick in-and-out rescue had taken a left turn. Not a problem. SEALs were always prepared. He radioed in to report the ambush while Phil and Cade pulled the rocket launcher out of the pack.

"Knock knock." Phil grinned.

Blake jackknifed into a sitting position. One fist rose in fury, the other slapped to his hip for his sidearm. But his hip was naked.

Just like the rest of him.

Shuddering, he swiped his forearm over the sweat trickling off his brow and took stock.

Naked. In bed. Sexy female body curled in the sheets next to him. Sunrise was peeking through uncurtained windows. Other than a long dresser and a stack of moving boxes, them and the bed, the room was empty.

Alexia's condo. Where he'd been for two incredible, sex-filled, erotically intense days. He turned his head. She was splayed across the satin sheet where she'd collapsed after their last round. Facedown, vivid red curls curtaining her face and shoulders, so only a hint of her rose tattoo peeked out, she was totally zoned. Given that they'd slept maybe a sum total of six of the last fifty-two hours, he wasn't surprised.

But he was grateful.

Wanting air, needing space, he carefully slid from the bed, grabbed his jeans and left the room. He skirted packing boxes, still lined and neatly labeled against the living-room wall. She hadn't been kidding when she said she'd just moved from New York. Most of her stuff, except a few large pieces of furniture, was still packed.

He was pretty sure she'd been here a week or two. Wouldn't most women have hit the boxes, hung the curtains, filled the space with doodads by now?

Not that they'd talked much, but he'd got the impression during one of their between-sex rest breaks that she wasn't in any hurry to settle in. Why? Missing New York? Not a fan of the California sun? He knew she'd lived here before, but not when. What'd made her leave? Was the job going to be enough to keep her here this time?

And why did he care so much?

Caring, wanting to know she'd be here long-term, curiosity about her past, her present, her future. Those were all off-limits. Bad ideas for a man who played Russian roulette for a living.

He crossed the cool living-room floor, his feet silent on the Mexican tiles, around the dining table and into the nook of a kitchen. A coffeepot, a single pan and a pair of wineglasses were all that were visible. He skipped the glass and stuck his head under the faucet, letting the cold water wash away the remnants of nausea his dream had caused.

He hadn't used sex to numb the memories, but if he'd been the type to do that kind of thing, it sure as hell hadn't worked. He shook the water off his hair, grabbing a paper towel to dry his face, and stared out the small window at the smaller garden beyond. Bright tropical-looking flowers bloomed, innocent and welcoming.

He felt happy and alive and filled with the weirdest sort of contentment with Alexia. She made him laugh. Watching her the few times she'd slept had filled him with a scary sort of peace. Her body was a wonderland, one he wanted to explore and lose himself in over and over again.

He didn't belong here.

He didn't do relationships, for one. And even though she'd made sounds like she wasn't looking for one either, she was the relationship kind of woman. Or maybe just the kind of woman who meant relationships to him.

He was due back on base the day after tomorrow. Most likely out of the country before the end of the week. And she didn't do navy guys. At least, Blake winced, she didn't when the guy was honest and up front before she'd done him.

Time to cut it short. Say goodbye, get back to real life. His gaze dropped from the view to his hands. Hands that just hours ago had been all over Alexia. Had touched, explored every inch of her delectable body. Hands that were as competent with a weapon as they were at bringing her to a screaming orgasm. Hands that *were* weapons.

He remembered the devastation on Phil's mom's face at the service. Blake's only comfort had been that nobody would be that torn up if he ended up in a flag-covered box. His only relation was his mom, who probably wouldn't sober up enough to attend. It was better that way.

Better not to get involved with someone. Not to ask them to risk caring, to risk being hurt.

Easier.

ALEXIA WOKE with a slow, moaning sort of sigh. Every muscle, every inch of her body was soaked in satisfaction.

She could barely move, and wasn't even sure she wanted to wake. Except in sleep, she'd miss out on the fun and games. And she really, *really* liked fun and games with Blake.

With a soft, purring sort of moan, she rolled onto her back, shoved her hair out of her face and scanned the bed. The wide, empty expanse of bed.

She frowned. Where *was* Blake? His belt was still draped over her dresser handle, and his shoes there by the door. She should go look for him, but she needed a break. Time to figure out why she felt so empty waking without him next to her.

That was stupid, she told herself. He was a one-night guy who'd simply extended the party a little. She wasn't going to be a cliché and start wishing he'd ask for more. They'd both made it clear that wasn't what they wanted. And she'd be damned if she'd be the one to renege on that. Of course, if he happened to have changed his mind, she wouldn't say no, either.

Shoving her hand through her hair again, she tugged the curls a few times, hoping it'd shake loose some of the confusion. That her thoughts would line neatly up into nice, manageable rows the way they were supposed to.

Maybe if they talked?

But she'd noticed that Blake wasn't much of a talking kind of guy. Maybe because his mouth had been so busy doing other things. Delightful things. Deliciously wonderfully sexual things.

Whew. Alexia waved her hand in front of her face. Shower time. Hopefully the cool water would chill down her thoughts, and her body, so she could focus.

Climbing from the bed with less grace than usual, she winced at the delicious soreness between her thighs. Clearly, her gym workouts didn't address toning hot, wild sex muscles. The few feet to the bathroom sent new tingles of pleasure through her. Her body a vivid reminder of why she was on them, she took her birth-control pill. As she reached for the spigot in the shower, she caught sight of her reflection.

Her hair was a red halo, framing a face that almost glowed with residual ecstasy. Her lips were swollen, eyes heavy. Whisker rash spread over her entire torso and lower, below the mirror's view, like a sunburn. Proof that there wasn't an inch of her body that Blake hadn't kissed. Worshipped. Pleasured in ways she'd only read about.

With a shuddering breath, she flipped on the spigot, not bothering with the hot water.

Thirty minutes, and not a few shivers, later, she made her way down the hallway with a frown. Why hadn't Blake come in? Not that she thought she was so irresistible that he couldn't keep his hands off her for the time it took to shower, but still…

She stepped into the still-unfamiliar living room. Tension she hadn't even realized was knotted in her shoulders unraveled. There he was at the table, reading the paper with his bare feet propped on a chair. Bare feet didn't scream *time to run away,* did they?

"Hey," he greeted. He folded the newspaper and smiled. Friendly enough, but Alexia suddenly felt as if she was under the icy-cold shower again. "I figured on letting you sleep awhile. You must be pretty worn-out."

"That's sweet," she decided, belting her robe tighter and moving into the center of the room. Did she give him a kiss? Just act casual? She wasn't sure. "But you haven't had much sleep, either. Aren't you tired?"

"I'm used to going without."

For his job? Because he didn't like to sleep?

"Why?"

He got to his feet, offered a half shrug and a smile, then reached out to pull her into his arms.

"Good morning," he murmured just before his lips covered hers.

Alexia forgot her question—hell, she forgot her name— as his mouth took hers in a slow, decadent morning dance of delight.

"You hungry?" he asked against her lips.

"Hungry?"

"Yeah. I'm starving. I figured I'd wait to make us both something. You ready to eat?"

"Um, sure." She stood there, a little confused, as he pressed a quick kiss to the tip of her nose, then released her to head into the kitchen.

Food was good. It was a nice, nonsexual way to spend time together, she told herself, wandering after him into the kitchen.

Her toes barely touched the linoleum when he turned and waved her back.

"Have a seat, relax. Read the paper. I've got this."

A guy who cooked and didn't expect—or want—help? Well, well. Too surprised to protest, Alexia turned right back around and made her way to the couch. Once there, she still didn't know what to say. He'd booted her out of her own kitchen. To cook for her. Should she be irritated or thrilled?

For a woman who prided herself on her communication skills, she was having some definite issues figuring out how to converse with Blake. Of course, the fact that she couldn't figure out how she felt about any single thing probably didn't help.

Might as well quit worrying and just enjoy the experience, she finally decided.

As delicious as two days of naked romping, rolling and

rocking were, even rabbits had to take a break from time to time. Knees a little weak as she recalled their last naked, rolling romp, Alexia snuggled deeper into her silk robe and watched Blake scramble eggs.

What was sexier? A man in the kitchen whipping up something delicious and nutritious? Or the sight of him, jeans unsnapped and slung low on his slim, tanned hips. *Oh, baby.* Alexia sighed, propping her chin on her fist. The man's body was a thing of beauty. Pure muscle, with not an ounce of fat anywhere. His shoulders were wide, his skin golden in the morning sunlight that streamed through her kitchen window.

"I didn't even realize I had eggs in the refrigerator," she said, her brain starting to awaken from its sexual stupor. She tore her gaze off his body to look at the counter between the condo's living room and kitchen. Orange juice, toast, a bowl of grapes. "Did you go to the grocery store?"

"Just next door," he said. "I borrowed some food from your neighbor."

Then he turned, frying pan in hand, to face her. Alexia actually felt her brain sputter as it sank under the waves of sexual heat again.

"I'm sorry. I should have had something here to feed you. A guest having to forage for his own breakfast fixings? That's a loss of major hostess points." She felt guilty as she slid to her feet. His eyes narrowed, locked on her body, then heated. Suddenly aware that her robe was gaping open, Alexia adjusted it with trembling fingers. Her breath hitched. Her pulse raced.

She'd lost count of the number of orgasms they'd shared, the multitude of ways they'd pleasured each other's bodies. She shouldn't be reacting like this. So hot, so easy. Shouldn't she know more about him before feeling so much more than desire? Shouldn't they have spent a lot more time together, clothed, before she started wishing he'd be giving her Halloween orgasms and Christmas orgasms and oh, please, Valentine's orgasms?

"I like cooking. Besides, you fed me dinner last night," he said with a shrug, dismissing the guilty apology she'd almost forgot she'd issued before diving down the emotional rabbit hole of worry.

He divvied eggs onto two plates, added toast and pushed them across the counter. Alexia frowned at the unspoken command—the guy was good at that—but picked them up and placed them on the table anyway. She came around the counter to get silverware while he carried juice and fruit to the table and sat.

"I fed you leftover fettuccine and steamed vegetables out of a freezer bag," she said with a laugh as she added forks to their plates. She pulled out a chair, but before she could sit, he grabbed her by the waist and swung her onto his lap.

Giggling, delighted, Alexia wrapped her hands behind his neck and tilted her head to the side. Her still-damp hair was chilly against her bare skin where the robe gaped yet again.

His eyes darkened to a midnight hue, narrowed with desire. She knew that look now. Knew the promise of it. Blake was demanding in bed. And in the shower. And on the balcony at two in the morning. Wherever their love-making took place, it was as if he grabbed inside her, took every bit of pleasure she could offer and then found a way to give her even more.

"I'll bet eggs would taste good eaten off your belly, too," he said, his voice low and husky against the sensitive curve where her shoulder met her throat. "Those noodles were pretty tasty that way."

That's what a woman got for not having a supply of

chocolate and whipped cream on hand, Alexia thought ruefully. Cold noodles in gooey cheese and butter slurped off her skin.

She wrinkled her nose, ready to remind him what a failure that had been, tastewise, when he kissed her.

Deep, intense. Mind-blowing.

Alexia melted.

Slowly, her lips still clinging to his, he pulled back and arched one brow at his plate.

She wasn't sure why she didn't want to. She had no idea where the strength to resist came from, but suddenly it seemed like the most important thing in the world. She needed a little distance, she realized. Some space to get a grip on this…what? It wasn't a relationship, was it? She didn't even know his last name. Had no idea what he did for a living. It wasn't as if the last two days had been silent. They'd shared plenty of words. It was just that most of them were in the form of directions, dirty talk or cries of ecstasy.

"I'd hate to ruin the taste of the eggs with the flavor of my body wash," she said, giving a little laugh as if it was a joke instead of a blatant excuse.

Blake didn't complain, though. Nor did he push the issue. He simply smiled, let her go and picked up his fork. He waited until she was seated before digging into the eggs on his plate.

The man was perfect. How was that possible?

It wasn't.

She settled in her chair, the brush of their knees sending sexual tingles up her thighs to tease her still-quivering flesh.

"Where are you from?" she asked after a few bites. She was suddenly aware that while she knew just how much pressure he liked when she stroked him, and how sucking on his tongue made him crazy, that was about the extent of her knowledge. "Are you a California boy?"

"No. I grew up in South Carolina, but now I'm more of a nomad."

She waited. But that was it. He didn't expand, he didn't explain. He just scooped up another forkful of eggs.

What the hell?

"A nomad, hmm? Does that mean you're just visiting, or will you be around awhile?"

He finished the last of his eggs, then gave her plate a questioning look. Alexia obediently forked up some of her own while he munched on toast.

"I'm here for a while," he said. "I like the weather in Southern California."

"And we have great beaches," she said with a smile, remembering where they first met. And, she quivered a little, where they first made love.

He didn't smile back, though. His gaze darkened, then shifted. As if someone had slammed the book shut. The pain she'd sensed in the bar was there again, radiating from him like a silent sob of misery.

They'd spent two days sharing their bodies. Surely he'd share this with her, too.

She wanted to ask him what was hurting him so deeply, why he was hiding from it. Before she could find the words, he gave her a wicked look, then reached one finger into the jelly bowl and scooped out a dollop of glistening orange sweetness.

"Taste?" he asked, offering her his finger. "Your neighbor said it's plum. Made from her own trees."

Beneath the amusement in his eyes was a challenge. Purely sexual, totally tempting. She couldn't resist. Alexia leaned forward, sucking the tip of his finger into her mouth. Yum. The sticky sweetness had a tart edge. As she swirled her tongue around, licking all the way to the knuckle, his gaze deepened. Intensified.

"More?" he asked, his voice husky.

Power, unlike anything she'd ever felt before, filled Alexia. This man had had her six ways from Sunday. He'd climaxed more times than she was years old. And he'd done it on barely any sleep. Yet just the swipe of her tongue, and he was all hot and bothered.

Totally turned on.

She stood, arched both brows, then unbelted her robe.

All it took was a shrug for it to drop to the floor.

"Gorgeous," Blake moaned in delight. He leaned forward to pull her onto his lap, but Alexia shook her head. Nope, it was her turn to call the shots.

"Strip," she ordered.

He grinned. Then, proving he was all for equality among the sexes when it came to loveplay, he stood, and in a few quick moves, had that incredible body bared for her pleasure.

Alexia dipped her fingers into the jelly jar, then smoothed them over his lower lip. With a delicate swipe of her tongue, she licked it clean.

"Yum," she told him.

He grinned, waiting to see what she'd taste next.

She swirled the sweet jelly around his nipples. Then she sucked them clean. They tightened gratifyingly, first one then the other, beneath her lips. She smoothed her other hand down his slender hips, over the rock-hard angles of his sexy butt.

She dipped her fingers in the jelly again, dropped to her knees and kissed her way down his belly. His body was a feast. Every inch delicious. And she wanted to taste him all.

"Nope," he said with a strained laugh, grabbing her

sticky fingers just before they could spread the breakfast preserve over his erection. "That'd get in the way of what I have planned next."

"But I wanted to taste," she said with a naughty smile. Her hand still in his, she leaned down to blow a soft puff of air on the glistening tip of his dick.

It jumped.

She slid a glance up at Blake, noting the hazy, almost-stupefied-with-wanting look on his face. Still, though, he didn't release her hand.

So she tasted without jelly.

First with just her tongue, sipping gently at the tip of his dick. Then she slid it down the hard length, and back up. His fingers, wrapped around her wrist, trembled. She sucked the velvety rounded tip. Just the tip. He groaned out loud.

Before she could take his entire delicious length into her mouth, he used her wrist to pull her to her feet. Her breath shocked right out of her, Alexia gasped. Still holding her hand, he lifted the jelly-smeared finger to his mouth and licked it clean. Then he grabbed her by the waist, flipped her around and pressed her body between his and the table.

"You're the most delicious woman in the world," he murmured against the back of her neck, his lips moving along her shoulder in soft, wet kisses. Both hands reached around, cupping her breasts. Fingers tweaked, pulled, swirled the tips until they ached with pleasure. Her butt brushed his erection again and again as her hips undulated, desperate for release. Wanting more, and since his hands were busy, she pressed her own down between her thighs, preparing, readying herself for the delight she knew he'd give.

"Mine," he protested, one of his hands sliding down to

cover hers, twining their fingers together so they worked the aching swollen nub in concert.

Alexia moaned, heat swirling, passion building tight in her belly. Before she could climb too high, too fast, Blake bent her low over the table.

Her face nestled in her arms, she let him position her, lifting her hips for his entry. Even with proof so many times over of how big, strong and fabulous he felt inside, she still gasped with shock when, his hands braced on her hips, he plunged deep.

Her fingers dug into the tabletop, the wood cool and unyielding under her. Her hips shifted. Back, forth and back again, meeting his thrusts.

One hand still guiding her hips, he slid the other between her thighs, flicking his finger over the quivering bud there.

She cried out with pleasure.

He thrust again. Flicked once more.

Two strokes, then three. Her body exploded. Stars danced a wild boogie behind her closed eyelids as she gasped, moaning his name over and over. The orgasm rocked her, her body pressing tighter to the table, to his hips, as if she could somehow wring even more pleasure from the climax.

Her moves were all the encouragement he needed. Blake's fingers dug into her hips, holding her still for his body. With a guttural moan, he plunged again, then once more. Then he groaned, loud and long. His thighs, so hard and strong, quivered against the back of hers.

Spent, totally empty, her body lay across the table as she tried to catch her breath. To find her thoughts. To remember her name.

"I have to go," Blake murmured, his lips brushing her

shoulder, making her shudder as yet another tiny orgasm rocked her body.

"No," she protested. She wanted to lift her head, to roll over and grab on to him. But she didn't have the strength. There was nothing left, he'd drained her dry.

She heard him move away but still couldn't open her eyes.

"Look, I've got a thing tonight," he told her. His voice was distant, as if he was trying to put space between them. A hint of panic flamed in her stomach. Before it could grow, he continued, "But I should be done by eleven, midnight at the latest. I'll come back."

Alexia's lashes fluttered. She forced her head to turn so she could see him. She wanted to protest. To tell him to ask instead of inform.

She might even have plans.

Her brow furrowed.

Wait.

She did have plans.

"I'm busy tonight," she realized, not sure which she wanted more. To exert herself, proving that this was a two-way street and she'd be calling just as many shots as he would. Or to grab on to an excuse to ditch the admiral's retirement party and have another bout of mind-blowing sex.

"How busy?"

She sighed. She'd promised Michael she'd be there. And she'd promised herself that if she moved back, she'd make her best effort to get along with her parents.

"Very busy." Pulling a face at having to climb off the cloud of sexual nirvana, she rolled to her side. Blake's eyes heated to blue flames. "I've got a family thing going on."

She only hesitated a second before adding, "But I can be back by midnight."

He zipped his jeans, tucking his T-shirt in and giving

her a long, contemplative look. As if he knew exactly what she was offering. Not just sex. Trust. A chance to see where this went. And, she admitted to herself with a sigh, rolling off the table, a boatload of expectations.

She could see the hesitation in his blue eyes. Knew he was weighing all that, probably against how fast he could hit the door. He stepped forward, sliding between her legs again and resting his hands on her bare waist.

Eyes open, staring into hers, he leaned down to meet her lips. Whisper soft, it was a promise, an acceptance. For the first time, his kiss didn't make her think, *Let's get naked*. It made her think, *Wow, there goes my heart*.

"Midnight, then," he said, kissing her one more time before striding to the door.

And just like that, she felt committed. She didn't know anything about him other than his name, that he was incredible in bed and that she'd trust him with her life.

Trust. That was the biggie.

Other than Michael, had she ever trusted another man in her life? Growing up with an emotionally—and often physically—absent father who ruled everything on a need-to-know basis, and a mother who didn't bother sharing important things like when or where they'd be moving next because she hadn't wanted to hear the whining, Alexia tended to demand a lot of information from people. Maybe it made her a little bit of a control freak, but she liked to know everything she could, before she made decisions.

And here she was, with a man who hadn't told her anything.

Alexia pressed her fingers to her lips, still sticky with plum jelly. The front door shut behind Blake.

"It's a date," she whispered to the empty room.

6

"Cheers, buddy," Cade said, tilting his beer—in a glass, no tacky bottles at the admiral's retirement party—against Blake's. The sound was lost in the sea of well-modulated voices, yawn-worthy chamber music and the almost silent white noise of the air conditioner. "Gotta admit, the old guy has style."

Blake shrugged. He'd grown up poor enough to appreciate that using a glass instead of the bottle gave the guy doing dishes a chance to earn a living. But other than that, opulence confused more than impressed him. What was the point? Rich people were more worried about showing off their fancy than guys were showing off the size of their…muscles.

He didn't bother saying that to Cade, though. Compared to the Sullivans, Cade's family, Admiral Pierce might as well move into the trailer park Blake had grown up in.

"What do you think he's gonna do now that he's retired?" Cade asked idly, his mellow tone at odds with the sharp intensity of his gaze as he scanned the crowd. "Put on one of those flowered shirts and putter in the garden?"

"I hope someone takes pictures," Blake snorted. Then, after another drink, he shrugged. "He's mentioned doing consults in D.C., maybe put together some programs here on the base."

That was the great thing about Cade. No pissiness over Blake having an inside track with the admiral. Then again, Cade's uncle was a senator and his father owned half of northern California. So he had plenty of inside tracks of his own.

"Why bother to retire, then?" Cade asked. "Retirement is supposed to be relaxing, isn't it? Like R&R every day?"

Blake grimaced. That was way too much relaxing for him. Like this party, that kind of deal just wasn't in his cards. He scanned the crowd again, looking for a waiter and another beer.

Unlike the poor civilian saps in tuxes, he and Cade, along with a bunch of bright shiny brass, got to wear their dress whites. It wasn't fatigues, but close enough to keep him comfortable.

"Sir," the waiter said with a little bow as he exchanged Blake's empty glass for a full one.

He shifted his shoulders against the constricting fabric. At least he used to be comfortable. For the first time since he'd put it on, it felt as if his uniform didn't fit right.

"What's up?" Cade asked after exchanging his own glass. "You've been antsy as hell all night."

"Just want to get out of here. This isn't my kind of thing."

"Dude, ya gotta party while the music's playing."

Cade's grin disappeared as the words cleared his mouth. That'd been Phil's favorite saying.

Blake stared into his own pilsner glass. They were trained for this. They went into every single mission knowing it wasn't just a possibility, but a probability, that sooner or later one of them wouldn't make it out. So what was with the emotional drama? When did it get easier?

"Landon, Sullivan, glad you could make it," the admiral said in a big, hearty social voice. As opposed to the big, gruff commanding voice he usually used to bark out orders. There actually wasn't a whole lot of difference in the two, except the slightly disturbing smile on his face.

"Congratulations on your retirement, sir," Cade said. "The base won't be the same without you."

You had to hand it to him, Cade rocked this social bullshit. And the admiral ate it up with a spoon.

"I did my best to leave a strong mark," he claimed before giving Blake an indulgent look that made the hairs on the back of his neck stand up. "And I like to think I'm leaving behind a legacy. That my influence will carry on, if you know what I mean."

"The mark of a great leader is the impact he leaves on his troops," Cade agreed.

Blake didn't have to look at him to know that beneath his social tone, his buddy was smirking.

"And speaking of legacies," the admiral said, pulling on that social smile again, "Landon, there's someone I'd like to introduce you to."

"Sir?" Shit. He didn't want to meet anyone.

"My daughter. A lovely young woman. Articulate, bright and gainfully employed. Top-security clearance, a solid portfolio, and being my daughter, she's well versed in what's required to support a military household."

Obviously Pierce didn't play matchmaker very often.

And Blake wished like hell he wasn't doing it now. He wasn't stupid. He knew what game the admiral was playing. The old guy liked Blake's story. SEAL, linguist, decorated soldier triumphing over a pathetic childhood. The son-in-law ad practically wrote itself.

Except Blake wasn't in the market.

"I'm sorry, sir," Blake said. "I'd be happy to make your

daughter's acquaintance, but I won't be asking her out. I'm seeing someone."

It wasn't until he saw the shock on his superior's face that Blake realized this was the first time he'd said no. His shoulders twitched again. It wasn't as if he'd refused an order, he told himself. All he'd done was sidestep the questionable honor of being dangled in front of the admiral's daughter.

"Elliot, darling," Mrs. Pierce said, giving Blake an apologetic smile before dismissing him with a tilt of her head. "It's time for the toast."

"Excellent," Pierce said, arching his brow at Blake. "You'll wait, of course. I'd like to finish this discussion."

Blake almost saluted out of habit.

"I'm a soldier, not a lapdog," he muttered instead as soon as the old guy was out of earshot.

"What's the big deal? You meet his daughter, play nice, then skip out to hook up with that hot redhead again."

Blake frowned.

"What? You didn't think I could figure out why you've been mooning all night?" Cade laughed. "Dude, it's practically written on your face. I'm surprised you can drink that beer with the hook stuck so tight in your lip."

Like feeding jackals, denial was pointless. Besides, Blake shifted uncomfortably, he wasn't a hundred percent sure that he wasn't hooked good.

He was spared the need to think of a comeback thanks to a chiming crystal bell.

First time he'd ever been grateful for a speech.

The gratitude lasted about five minutes.

"I hate politics," Blake decided under his breath, not for the first time.

"You want to get anywhere, get anything done, you play the game." Cade shrugged as though it didn't matter. But his lips twisted, a bitter indication that he, too, thought the game sucked.

Blake ignored the droning accolades, letting his mind wander back to Alexia. As soon as this toast was over—regardless of who the admiral wanted him to meet—he was outta there. He wanted to see her. To talk to her. To taste and touch and have her.

No surprise, really, since he hadn't been able to get her out of his mind. Except the wanting to talk to part. That could probably be filed under shocking.

But as hot as things were between them, he knew she wasn't going to be satisfied with just sex much longer. She'd already been pushing, hinting. He remembered the aggravation in her eyes that morning. She wanted more, and if he wanted her, he was going to have to pony up.

He shifted, his uniform suddenly tightening like a strait-jacket. Sharing his past wasn't an issue. Admitting his job? It was going to take a whole lot of charm to get her naked after he fessed up to being not only navy, but a SEAL, too.

He was pretty sure he had enough, though.

"Well, now…" Cade murmured, his grin wicked.

Blake followed his gaze.

He recognized the man first. Strawberry-blond hair fashionably tousled, alligator tuxedo lapels indicating not just custom, but way-out-there custom, and a ruby pinkie ring that glinted as he waved a friendly greeting to the crowd.

Michael?

What was he doing here? Was he a part of the entertainment? Blake wondered what he'd missed while he was obsessing over Alexia.

He watched the younger man reach out to assist someone onto the raised dais. His hand closed over slender fingers. It took an obvious tug to get the rest of the woman's body to move. Despite his confusion, Blake grinned. Somebody didn't like the spotlight.

Then, as people shifted, he saw who Michael was trying to drag onstage.

Her hair tumbled in loose curls over one bare shoulder, the red so deep it was almost black in places, so light it shone gold in others. Something black draped a tall, willowy body, the effect saved from elegance by the slender rose tattooed on her bare shoulder. The fabric was deceptively loose, but wrapped in a way that drew his eyes to the sweet curve of her breasts, the slender indention of her waist.

Breasts he'd tasted just hours before. A waist he'd gripped as he'd held her body over his, watching as she slid in a glorious rhythm, up and down his straining erection.

Alexia.

His sexy temptation.

His gaze shifted from her to the man of the hour, suddenly seeing the resemblance in the shape of their faces, the arch of their brows.

The tiny hairs on the back of his neck that warned of trouble stood on end.

Alexia was the admiral's daughter?

Shit.

STANDING ON DISPLAY, Alexia kept her expression neutral and her shoulders erect. She hated these things. Her mother was as social as the admiral was bossy, which meant growing up there had been four over-the-top fancy functions a year.

Since Margaret Pierce came from money—lots and lots of money—that meant the parties were not only boring, but super-upscale boring. The only upside was that events on this scale meant that other than assuring themselves their offspring were in attendance and properly behaved, the admiral and Mrs. Pierce were too busy to do anything but ignore them all night.

When it came to her parents, Alexia usually believed that being ignored was best. But she'd forgotten how hellishly boring it was.

"Hide the ennui," Michael whispered. Thanks to her heels, he only had to lean sideways, so the exchange wasn't that noticeable. Good thing, since their mother was a stickler for social protocol.

"I'm swimming in ennui," she whispered back, her lips barely moving from their frozen smile.

Actually, she was swimming in anticipation. She glanced at the ornate grandfather clock on the landing and sighed. Only an hour till midnight. That meant a few boring speeches, a couple ostentatious odes to her father's brilliance, and whatever pompous response he ended the toast with, and she could leave.

Go back to her place and wait for Blake.

She'd been so amped up after he'd left, she'd finally dug into the packing boxes. Sure, she'd opened the first one in search of her favorite teddy, a confection of black lace and red satin. But within a few hours, she'd turned her barren bedroom into a comfortable oasis. One she'd be happy to spend another two days of sexual ecstasy in.

The image of Blake popped into her mind, his eyes intense, his incredible body poised over hers. So delicious.

She sighed, a soft fog of sexual warmth wrapping around her as it always did when she pictured the two of them together.

She couldn't wait to touch him again. To feel his body inside her. To taste the intense heat of his kisses. But first, before she let herself have any of that, the two of them would be sitting down for a little chat.

Because as wonderful as things were between them, she wasn't having sex with a stranger again. And, despite the fact that she now knew his body as well as she did her own, facts were facts. Blake was an *emotional* stranger to her.

"Why isn't Dr. Darling here to distract you?"

Guilt, sharp and cutting, sliced through Alexia's sexual fog. She had no reason to feel bad. There was no commitment between her and Edward, either concrete or implicit. It was stupid to feel guilty. Just because she'd spent the previous couple of nights rolling around naked in the sand, surf and sheets with the hottest, sexiest, most passionate man she'd ever met instead of calling the guy who wanted her to be his one and only?

She winced. Nope. No reason for guilt.

Michael's nudge reminded her that he was waiting for an answer. Since this probably wasn't the right moment to share her emotional confusion, she shrugged and went for humor instead.

"Are you kidding? Bring a date to a family affair?" she whispered back in mock horror. "That's never a good idea."

"It'd help you decide if you want to take the relationship plunge, though," Michael mused quietly. "What better way to see what a guy's made of than let him go up against the old man? If he caves, you know he's a wimp. If he cozies up, you know he's an ass."

Alexia shrugged. The only measure of her father she cared about was that any guy she was in a relationship with was nothing like the man who'd sired her. Other than that, she didn't care how he acted around the admiral.

She was just about to ask Michael to run interference once the toast ended—so she could slide out the door— when she caught the steely disapproval in her mother's stare. Alexia subtly nudged her brother, who straightened, too, both of them shifting their fake-smiling faces toward center ring as their father started speaking.

As the cadence shifted, winding down, she felt some of the tension seeping from her shoulders, out her fingers. They were in the end zone. She focused in on the words, listening to her father thank a laundry list of dignitaries, ranking officers and political cronies for their support of his career over the last four decades.

She leaned toward Michael.

"Think he'll include us?" she whispered.

"Nah," he whispered back. "The only time we come up in a speech is in terms of the challenges and struggles he's had to overcome."

"As soon as this is over, I'm outta here," she muttered.

"Not so fast. Remember, we're part of the receiving line. You have to stand and smile until everyone's done worshipping—I mean, congratulating Dad. Besides, you should stick around." Michael's smile was pure delight. "I'll bet your night improves."

"I'm sure it will."

Just as soon as she got out of here and called Blake. She surreptitiously glanced at the grandfather clock in the corner, noting it was already eleven-thirty.

Why couldn't her father have toasted goodbye to all his glory at a reasonable hour, instead of pushing it to the limits and forcing everyone to stay so late? She glanced around. Most of the guests were pretty darned old. They probably wanted warm milk and their beds instead of a boring speech and champagne.

Skimming the crowd, her gaze flew right past one particular face. Then, her brain screaming a warning, her eyes flew back so fast she probably lost a few lashes.

Blake?

Brow furrowed, she shook her head in denial.

What was he doing here?

Then her focus widened. Horror filled her with a cold, icy sort of misery.

No!

Her eyes bounced from his uniform to the medals glinting off his chest, back to his face and then to the crowd of men he was standing with. SEALs.

Navy SEALs.

The man who'd driven her crazy, who had her thinking forever thoughts and craving a relationship, the one who made her want to play house—naked—was also the one thing, the only thing, on her forbidden-relationship list. Military. Elite military, and up until one speech ago, under her father's command.

How had she missed the signs?

Why hadn't he told her?

And when the hell would these speeches be over so she could run away?

BLAKE WATCHED the expressions chase across Alexia's face. Shock, then disbelief, quickly followed by fury. Then she shifted. Her body weight, the tilt of her head and her expression. It was as if she'd slammed the door shut.

Shit.

As much as he wanted to avoid any matchmaking from the admiral, he was equally determined to hold on to the sweet, pleasurable oblivion Alexia's body provided.

Hurry, hurry, hurry, he silently urged his commanding officer, knowing the longer Alexia had to stew, the harder it would be to charm her out of her snit.

Thankfully, the older man chose that moment to raise his glass in thanks. Blake absently followed along with the rest of the room, raising his, as well. But his eyes didn't leave Alexia.

A good thing, because as soon as the crowd shifted, she lost herself in it. Clearly, growing up with military influence had taught her a thing or two.

Of course, Blake had some pretty solid training on his side. He noted the direction she was going, then skirted the outside of the crowd, cutting her off before she reached the door.

He placed his hand on her shoulder with just enough pressure to stop her escape. She hissed, a sound like cold water being thrown on a sizzling fire.

Blake dropped his hand.

"Surprise," he said quietly, suddenly very aware that they were surrounded by her family and his superiors. None of whom needed any details as to his and Alexia's relationship. "I didn't realize you were Admiral Pierce's daughter."

"And I didn't realize it mattered who my father was." Her tone was as cold as her eyes. A temperature he'd have sworn a woman as hot as she was could never drop to.

"It doesn't," he said, dancing out of that trap. Alert, knowing there were more to come, he weighed his words carefully. "I hadn't realized we had mutual interests."

She gave him a long, considering look that made him wish he was in combat gear.

"I hadn't, either. That's one of those things that usually comes up in conversation. Which is another thing we never had."

Blake shifted to block her exit again.

"Where are you going?" he asked.

"Away."

Blake had swum through the Arctic Ocean once and swore it'd been warmer than her tone. Brows arched, he gestured to the open French doors.

"Why not go this way, then?" he suggested. "We can talk."

"No." Lips pressed so tight together they were white at the edges, she took a long, deep breath through her nose, then exhaled slowly. "No, thank you. I'd rather not go out on the patio. I'd rather not talk. I prefer to go home."

"I'll go with you."

"I prefer to go alone."

Before Blake could counter that, they were interrupted.

"Lieutenant," the admiral greeted with the biggest smile Blake had ever seen on his face. The empty champagne flute in his hand might factor in, but retirement probably didn't hurt.

"Sir." Blake shifted aside just a little so the older man could talk to his daughter. But instead of words, Pierce's smile dimmed and all he offered his daughter was a nod.

Then, proving that a dozen or so toasts hadn't affected his perception, his gaze shifted back and forth between them. "The two of you have met already?"

Blake waited for Alexia to answer.

"We said hello on the beach last week," she finally told her father.

"And?"

"And, nothing." Her words were as flat as her expression. Blake didn't get it. Alexia was unquestionably the brightest woman he'd ever met. Not just smart, although he was pretty sure she topped that chart, too. But bright in energy, in color. With her vivid red curls, her expressive face and her enthusiasm, she shone like neon.

Until now.

The color was still there. Her hair as red, her eyes as brown. Her smile, painted a vivid rusty rose, didn't alter. But she looked as if someone had flipped a switch and shut her down. Turned her off.

The last thing a woman like Alexia was meant to be was off.

Even pissed at him, she'd still shot off a few sparks. Like a woman with a fabulous temper who'd learned to control it. But now? Blake's gaze cut from her to the admiral, then back. What the hell was going on?

"I told you to plan on staying for at least an hour after the address to perform some specific social duties I required," the admiral informed his daughter, his gaze shifting from her face to her purse, clutched in white fingers, and then to the door.

"And I told you that I was here to celebrate your retirement, as mother requested. But that I'd have to leave as soon as the address was finished."

Blake was starting to get the impression that this wasn't a loving father-daughter relationship.

"I gave you an order, young lady. I expect it to be obeyed." The admiral gestured to Blake. "Luckily, the two of you have already broken the ice. Lieutenant Landon is one of my protégés. I'd like you to spend some time getting to know each other."

And there it was—Blake sighed—the last nail in his coffin.

He stepped forward, surreptitiously putting himself between father and daughter. Before he could defuse the situation, Alexia gave a chilly smile and shook her head.

"I'm sorry. We've spent enough time getting to know each other already and discovered we're completely incompatible. Now, if you'll excuse me…?"

Her icy smile skated over both of them before she turned heel and walked out.

Just walked right out the door.

It was a toss-up who was more shocked.

Blake, or her father.

Looked as if he didn't have quite as much charm as he'd thought.

"Excuse me," the admiral said stiffly before following her. Blake deemed it wise to stay where he was. Neither would welcome his presence at this point.

But he wasn't willing to let it go, let her go. Blake looked around.

There.

He made his way across the room to a small cluster of people.

"Excuse me," he interrupted, not caring about protocol or manners at this point. "Michael, I need to speak with you."

Alexia's brother's eyes widened as he realized who Blake was. He did a visual up and down, taking in the uniform, then offered a morose shake of his head. "Yep, we should talk."

He cheerfully excused himself from the couple, then gestured toward the same door Blake had tried to get Alexia through earlier. At least one of the Pierce siblings was willing to take a walk under the moonlight with him.

"I didn't know you were navy," Michael said as soon as they cleared the French doors. With an elegant wave of his hand, he indicated they sit on the bench swing.

"Does it matter?" Blake asked, not wanting to sit since he saw this as more an interrogation than a friendly chat. Leaning comfortably against the wooden back, one foot cocked over his knee, Michael didn't seem to care.

"Not to me."

"But it matters to Alexia," Blake guessed. "Why didn't she say anything?"

"Well, it's not like you had an in-depth discussion there on the beach." Then he gave Blake a searching look, arched both brows and asked, "Unless you had a little tête-à-tête after the beach encounter?"

SEALs didn't break that easily. Apparently a denial or confirmation wasn't necessary. Michael gleefully dived right into conclusionville. "Ooh, this is juicy. Where did you hook up? And did you? Hook up, I mean? Obviously you did. No wonder she was all airy-fairy this evening. This is probably why she didn't want to bring Dr. Darling to the shindig."

"Who?"

"Some guy," Michael dismissed with another wave of his hand. "Doesn't matter. What matters are the details. When did you get together, where were you and what are your intentions? Those are the questions that need answering."

"What guy?" Blake persisted, shifting his body weight so he loomed rather than stood over the younger man. "What's his relationship with Alexia? Is she involved? Is he someone she cares about?"

"If she cared, he'd be here."

Blake rocked back on his heels.

He was here. But not with Alexia. There was a message in that somewhere.

"What's her issue with the military?"

"Well, you've met our father." For the first time, Michael's carefree facade cracked, showing a layer of bitter hurt. Blake had seen the same expression in Alexia's eyes in the bar, when she'd talked about military men. Seemed the admiral wasn't in the running for any father-of-the-year prizes.

"I'm sorry," Michael said, charm back in place as he got to his feet. "I really am. I think you'd be good for Alexia."

"So why are you sorry?"

"Because she won't talk to you again."

"You don't know that." Even though it was pretty much exactly what she'd said. But Blake didn't accept it. And what he didn't accept, he changed.

"Look, you're a great guy," Michael explained. "And Alexia deserves great, unquestionably. But she'll never date a soldier." He hesitated, as if he was worried about Blake's reaction. Then he laid a sympathetic hand on his shoulder. "I'm sorry."

Blake dropped to the bench swing as he watched the younger man walk away.

Up until three weeks ago, he'd loved his job. He'd trained for it, embraced it, lived for it. He'd never questioned being a SEAL. Never wanted anything else.

But in the space of the last couple of weeks, that same job he loved, he identified with, had taken two things that he hadn't wanted to give up.

His buddy.

And the most fascinating woman he'd ever met.

He couldn't do a damn thing about Phil. But he could about Alexia. All he needed was a plan, a little strategy and the right hook. He'd get her back.

Damned if he wouldn't.

7

BLAKE GAVE ALEXIA an hour. Enough time to chill, but not enough to stew. He used the time wisely, stopping by Cade's to change into jeans. She hadn't been kidding when she said she wasn't a fan of a guy in uniform.

Truce wasn't going to be negotiated if he pissed her off from the get-go. Not that he expected an easy surrender on her part. She was too fiery for that. Too intense. Which was just one of the reasons he was crazy about her.

One of the reasons he refused to let her end this between them.

Parking his truck in front of her condo, he took a breath. Middle-of-the-night battles had a different feel than daytime skirmishes. An edge.

Prepared to win, he strode up to her door and knocked.

He figured she'd be mad at first, probably have that chill going still. He'd charm her a little, play the apology game, bring her around to admitting that he hadn't done anything wrong. Five, ten minutes tops and he'd be reveling in the pleasure of her again.

A few seconds later he knocked again.

He didn't have to look at his watch to know it was

1:00 a.m. Just like he didn't have to look at her brightly lit windows to know she was still up.

He waited a few more seconds, then pulled out his cell phone and dialed.

"You might as well answer," he told her machine when it picked up. "I'll stay here all night. Patience is a particular virtue of mine, remember? I can last all night, babe. You know that. Even when you're naked, gyrating over me and driving me crazy, I can hold out. Actually, I like waiting. It's like a personal test, to see how many times I can make you come before I can't control myself anymore."

Before he could detail all the things he'd liked that she did to push that control, the door swung open. Blake grinned.

Alexia's glare was lethal.

Her hair, sleek and sexy just hours ago, was brushed out in a wild frizz so it haloed her face like an angry red cloud.

Her face was scrubbed clean, the siren's glow that'd matched her evening dress completely eradicated. All that was left was a sprinkling of freckles across her nose and smudged remnants of mascara under her furious eyes.

His lips twitched. Was this girl-battle 101? Make the enemy think they don't want the goods so they walk away without bothering to engage?

Nope.

His gaze skimmed the huge sweatshirt, noting that Jon Bon Jovi was still sporting the big curls and guyliner. The faded gray fabric enveloped her so well, her curves disappeared. Frayed cotton shorts drooped to her knees.

Her toenails were still a glittery, sexy red, though.

Her legs smooth and silky looking.

Her translucent skin flushed with anger, she was just as sexy now as she'd been wrapped in that tiny bikini on the beach.

Not a chance he'd walk away.

He wanted those goods.

"We need to talk," he said. The sooner they did, the sooner he could strip ole Jon off her body and get down to worshipping those toes.

"Talk? You know the concept?" she asked, not shifting out of the doorway.

"I've been introduced to it a time or two," he said drily. Figuring she'd negotiate better if she thought she was calling the shots, he didn't push her to let him inside. Instead, he leaned against the door frame and gave her a charming smile.

She automatically stepped back, glowered, then stood her ground again. Damn, she was cute.

"I think the opportunity to talk has passed. I'm sure, as a military man, you're aware of how many battles have been lost not because of mistakes, but because of timing."

Blake wasn't sure if it was because he knew Pierce was her father, or if it was her tone of voice, so precise, cold and similar to the admiral's, but the resemblance between them was remarkable at that moment.

"I don't let other people's mistakes dictate my decisions," he told her. "And I've never lost a battle."

"Well, you won't be able to say that again, will you?" she taunted with a chilly smile.

Blake's smile wavered for a second. He'd figured she'd be angry, but this was a little over the top.

"Would you mind clarifying something for me?" he asked, running low on charm. Not waiting for her response, he continued, "I didn't do anything wrong. I didn't lie to you, I didn't cheat my way into your bed. I didn't even make any promises. I was respectful, honorable and up-front."

He waited for her to acknowledge his largesse. Instead, she slammed her arms across her chest and glared.

Wow. Talk about standing guard over that mountain she'd constructed from a tiny pile of dirt.

"So, what's the deal?" he asked when he saw that's all he was going to get. "Why are you so angry?"

There.

The facts, simply laid out and incontrovertible.

He didn't expect an apology right away. He figured pride, the baffling twists of a woman's mind and maybe a little embarrassment at overreacting would have to be worked through first. He could wait.

His gaze skimmed her shapeless, colorless outfit again and his blood heated. He sure hoped she'd let him in so he could enjoy himself while he waited.

"Ah, those fine lines," she mused, relaxing enough to lean against the edge of the door she still gripped and crossing one ankle over the other. "The only problem with your argument is that you're ignoring intention. Communication isn't just the words we say, it's the message we intend to share."

"I don't want to sound crude, but what I intended to share was my body with yours. A good time, a lot of incredible sex and, as we spent more time together, maybe a chance to build more," he countered, reaching out to take her hand. He shoved his impatience back, telling himself this was part of what made her so appealing. Her fiery nature.

Then she moved her fingers away. His brow furrowed. But when she didn't close the door any farther he let himself start to relax. *Almost there.*

"Oh, yes, the wonders of sex. It was great, wasn't it?" she said, her smile wicked. He shifted, starting to feel a little nervous when it didn't reach her eyes. "And we both had the same intentions when it came to that. But one of us, unlike the other, hid pertinent facts in order to have all that great sex."

"I didn't hide a damn thing," he denied, starting to get irritated.

"No? You didn't hide your job, your lifestyle, your affiliation? Given that being a SEAL requires a level of dedication that's steeped in the blood, not sharing that was a deliberate choice on your part. Since I'd made my feelings about being involved with a military man clear, I can only assume that choice was made with the intention of hiding your career from me."

She sounded like a freaking lawyer. Or worse, he realized, gritting his teeth, a psychologist.

"You didn't share your last name," he countered.

"You're right." She inclined her head, the move sending her halo of frizzed-out curls wafting around her face. "And that makes me loose and easy. Which is still better than a liar in my book."

That was enough. Blake straightened, giving her a dark look. Name-calling? That's the best she could do?

"Look, you have some issues with your father. I get that. And I know he pissed you off with his little matchmaking game. But what does it matter? We're great together. You're not going to toss that away over him, are you? Because, what? You have some kind of Pavlovian response, automatically rejecting whatever your father approves of?"

As the words cleared his lips, Blake cringed.

She froze. Everything except her eyes. Those were like fire. She gave him a long, slow once-over before meeting his gaze again. This time he almost stepped back. "Well, aren't you clever? Throwing out those psych terms like an expert. Clearly you've got it all figured out. So tell me,

Blake… Do you know the meaning of closure? How about inductive reasoning? Or here's a simple one. Goodbye."

She didn't wait for his response before stepping back and slamming the door shut in his face.

Damn.

Furious with himself, Blake glared at the closed door.

He deserved to get shot down over that one.

Dammit, he'd just wanted a space from the memories, a chance to be a man instead of a soldier who'd just lost a brother-in-arms. What was it with women, always expecting a guy to spill his guts and blab like they did? He didn't want to talk about his job, or about Phil. He was escaping, not looking for a chance to wallow.

And if she'd wanted to know more about who he was, what he did for a living, then that was on her. She should have asked instead of pitching a fit after the fact.

He resisted the temptation to bang on the door again, shoving his fists in his pockets instead. Grinding his teeth, he stared unseeingly while his mind regrouped.

He wasn't finished.

He never gave up.

But, as much as it grated to admit, retreat was the only option right now.

Tomorrow, though?

Tomorrow, he'd win.

THE LAST THING Alexia wanted to do after a sleepless night spent crying over Blake was to face her father. She'd wanted to stay in bed with the covers pulled over her head and a bowl of hot fudge.

But she knew that walking out on his party was tantamount to a declaration of war. As with all conflicts the admiral oversaw, the battles would be played to win at all costs. But she'd spent her formative years learning strategy and figured she was as prepared as she could be.

She wouldn't win. Nope, she wasn't delusional. Going up against an admiral in the United States Navy, a SEAL trainer? She didn't stand a chance. This was all about mitigating damages.

The timing was crucial. A waiting period of just long enough for his temper to drop but not long enough for it to chill.

The combat zone had to be chosen with an eye toward tactics. Brunch at her mother's table didn't guarantee he wouldn't get ugly. But it did mean he'd have to stop to take sips of his coffee between insults.

Her weapons? Maturity and logic, and a gift for communication. As long as she kept her temper and presented her case in a diplomatic, intelligent way, the admiral would listen. He might not agree, but he'd listen.

So, there ya go, she told herself. *Ready to rock.*

Standing on her parents' porch, she pressed one hand to her churning stomach, said a little prayer and knocked.

She didn't recognize the housekeeper who answered, but followed her meekly down the hall. When they passed the French doors where she'd had her confrontation with Blake, she almost tripped over her own Jimmy Choos. Why'd he have to show up last night? Her eyes filled again, both fury and hurt making her want to hit something. It was like Cinderella at the ball, watching her prince turn into a rabid toad.

No. She clenched her fist around the strap of her purse and took a deep breath. This wasn't the time to think about Blake. All weaknesses, all worries, all distractions had to be ignored. Because eggs Benedict and mango aside, this was war.

"Mother," she greeted. Then, her fingers only trembling a little, she smiled at the admiral. "Father. Good morning."

"Alexia," her mother exclaimed. The older woman was perfectly made up. Her hair was more golden, like Michael's, than red like her daughter's, and fell in a smooth swing around a wrinkle-free face that didn't show a single sign of her late night. Ever the perfect hostess, she indicated to the housekeeper to bring in another plate even as she rose to give her daughter a kiss on the cheek. "What a lovely surprise."

"Lovely?" her father derided, snapping his newspaper shut and slapping it onto the table. He gave Alexia a dark look. "I had higher expectations of your moving back here, young lady."

For a second, just one sparkling bright second, Alexia's heart melted. He'd wanted her back? He'd anticipated her return?

"And this is how you behave now you're here? By insulting me and my guest?"

Silly heart, she chided, sliding into a chair and setting her purse at her feet to give herself time to blink away the unexpected tears.

"I'm sorry you saw it as an insult," she apologized when she looked up, her words sincere. "The last thing I wanted to do was hurt you."

She'd promised herself when she'd moved back to San Diego that she'd handle her relationship with her parents in a mature, dignified fashion. No hiding, no avoiding, no drama.

"I'm sure Alexia had a good reason for leaving," Margaret chimed in, irritation giving an extra snap to her words. "Let it be, Elliot. She's only been home a week, probably hasn't even unpacked yet. The last thing she needs right now is to worry about a relationship."

The tension ratcheting down a notch, Alexia gave her mother a grateful smile. It'd been rare growing up that their mother sided against their father. Allies must present a united front, after all.

"We'll have dinner next weekend," Margaret continued, gesturing to Alexia to have some fruit. "Just a quiet little get-together. You can invite the lieutenant then, Elliot."

Alexia's shoulders sagged. She fisted the crisp white fabric of her skirt between her fingers to keep from banging them on the table. She specialized in communication. Why could she never get through to her parents?

"I'm sorry, Mother," she tried again, calling on patience. "But I'm not interested in dating Lieutenant Landon. Not last night, not next week. Not ever."

"That's ridiculous," her father stated. "He's a fine young man. A great career ahead of him. You're just being stubborn out of habit."

"No. I'm trying to be clear. I've just moved to town and, as Mother said, haven't even unpacked yet. I start a new job tomorrow, one that's going to take all my focus and concentration. I'm not interested in a relationship right now."

At least, not anymore. She pressed her lips together to keep them from trembling. Yesterday, she'd been wide-open to the idea.

"Speaking of that job," the admiral said, propping his elbows on the table and giving her a steely look. "I'd like for you to meet with the head of the Dillard Institute next week. They have an opening for an acoustical engineer. Now that you have top-level clearance, you'd qualify just fine."

"I have a job already. One I moved across the country for." Stress did a grinding little twist in her gut as Alexia realized that her walking out the night before was only the opening salvo to her father's list of issues. He had a whole arsenal of complaints to shoot her way.

Her father waved away her objection. "You'll need to change jobs. Did you see today's paper? There's a write-up about you and that sex-research grant in there. It's completely unacceptable."

Unacceptable. How often had she heard that over the years? Closing her eyes, Alexia tried to breathe past the knot in her chest. Why had she expected things to change?

"Are you paying attention, young lady?"

He never used her name. Maybe he didn't know it. All her life, she'd been young lady. And for this, she was making herself ill? Worrying herself into misery, all while apologizing for making an adult choice in a matter that was completely her decision?

Alexia opened her eyes, lifted her napkin from her lap and set it on the table next to her plate. She gave her mother, then her father, a distant smile and got to her feet.

"Where do you think you're going?" he snapped.

"I'd hoped that in moving back we could heal our relationship. If not come to love and enjoy one another, at least reach a respectful camaraderie," she informed them in the same smooth, distant cadence she'd used delivering her dissertation at the age of twenty-two. "Unfortunately, in the handful of hours we've spent in each other's company I've come to realize that would be impossible."

"You're being dramatic," Margaret said with a sigh, topping her orange juice off with more champagne.

"No, Mother, I'm being practical." Alexia bent down to pick up her purse, then faced her father. "You've made it clear that I'll never be good enough to meet your standards."

"You mean you won't try to meet them."

"Since that would require that I date men you choose,

regardless of my feelings about them, and that I change my career to suit your preferences, then no. I won't."

"If you walk out that door, you're finished with this family." The admiral's voice was as emotionless as if he'd just recited the weather forecast. Of course, he probably figured the weather was more cooperative than his eldest child.

For the first time since she'd walked into her parents' house that morning, Alexia smiled. "That's the last thing you said to me when I graduated college and moved to New York."

She didn't wait for a response. There was no point.

THREE HOURS, FOUR IBUPROFEN and a cold compress later, Alexia lay on her couch practicing meditative breathing. The now-lukewarm cloth across her eyes dimmed the light while the soothing sounds of her relaxation tape played through her earbuds.

Suddenly, someone pressed a hand against her arm.

She screamed. Heart racing, she jackknifed. The damp terry cloth went flying one way, her iPod the other.

"Calm down," Michael said, both hands raised as if to prove he was unarmed. "It's just me."

"What're you doing here?" She eyed the cloth now hanging off the rosewood table, but didn't have the energy to move it. Instead, she dropped back to her pillow and tossed her forearm over her eyes.

"I heard you had brunch with the parents. So I brought ice cream."

Alexia shifted her arm just enough to peer out. Michael shook the white bag as proof.

"Your favorite. Double-chocolate caramel with almonds." He waited until she was upright before handing it to her. "The spoon's in the bag."

Chocolate might not fix everything, but it sure made suffering through it a lot easier, Alexia decided as she opened her treat.

"I can't believe I thought it would be different. How stupid is that?" She dug into the carton, pressing hard to fill her spoon.

"You aren't stupid. Most people have decent relationships with their parents. You probably just forgot that yours aren't human."

Alexia's lips twitched. Then she sighed, staring at the spoonful of chocolate for a few seconds before gulping it down. It was delicious, but didn't soothe the way it should.

"Besides, it's not the admiral and his Mrs. that has you all tweaked out."

"Well, aren't you the king of perception," she muttered.

"Queen, actually." Michael grinned. "And to prove it, I'll continue my brilliant assessment."

Alexia curled her feet under her and gestured with the spoon for him to have a go at it.

"You're upset about the hottie from the beach, right?"

Alexia gave a jerk of her shoulder, pouting into the carton instead of meeting her brother's gaze.

"You had fun with him?"

"Do hours and hours of mind-blowing sex count as fun?"

"They do in my book."

"Then sure. We had fun. But that's all it was. Fun."

"And what's wrong with that?"

"Nothing." Getting up because the chocolate was starting to hurt her stomach, not because she wanted to avoid any aspect of this fabulous conversation, Alexia headed into the kitchen. "Water?"

"Sure. While you get it, you can tell me what you were hoping for from Blake."

Honesty.

Openness.

Forty or so more orgasms.

A chance to build a relationship.

"Nothing," she said, pulling two bottles from the fridge and letting the cool air chill the heat on her cheeks. She'd never been a good liar.

"Well, then you got exactly what you wanted," Michael decided when she handed him his water. "Too bad he didn't get what he wanted."

Sure he had. On the beach. In his truck. On her bed. In her shower. Hell, right there on her dining-room table. He wasn't a shy, retiring sort of guy. If he'd wanted anything more than that, he'd have said so.

A bitter weight settled in her stomach.

"How would you know what he wanted?"

"After you left last night he found me."

Alexia's feet dropped to the floor. Wide-eyed, she peered at her brother, trying to see what he wasn't saying.

"And?"

"And you're awfully interested for a woman who wants nothing from him."

"Why'd he find you?" she pressed, ignoring the dig.

"To ask what it'd take to get you to talk to him again." Michael crossed one slender ankle over his khaki-clad knee and sipped his water, then arched one elegant brow. "So? What'll it take?"

"For him to change careers. To get amnesia and forget he served with Father. To learn the importance of open, honest communication."

"He's not going to change careers. He's a SEAL, he's totally dedicated. Would you change careers for a relationship? I think not," Michael said reasonably. She peered at him, wondering if he'd been hiding in the kitchen during brunch.

"Then we have no chance of being together," Alexia stated, getting to her feet to pace. "Because me dating a solider, a SEAL, at that, well, it'd be like you dating a woman."

"Eww." Michael grimaced. "No need to be gross."

"But you get what I mean, right?" She stopped in front of her brother and dropped down to sit on the coffee table. "It's not like it's a bad thing for someone else. I'm not dissing the military itself, or the idea of someone else dating soldiers."

"It's just not your thing."

"Exactly," she said, grateful that he understood.

"Except Blake? He is your thing," Michael pointed out gently. "You had fun with him. You connected. Great sex? That's not just physical. Once or twice, sure. But days on end? That's a connection, Alexia. Sometimes a once-in-a-lifetime kind of connection. Are you willing to let your prejudices stand in the way of that?"

She sighed. Dropping her gaze to her hands, she watched her fingers twist together. Remembered how they'd looked against Blake's tanned skin, smoothing, touching. Caressing.

It'd been incredible.

Could she risk it? He was the kind of guy who'd demand everything. She'd already experienced that firsthand when it came to sex. Physically, there was no holding back with Blake. He gave one hundred percent and demanded just as much in return.

But she needed more than just physical.

Only a week ago, she'd wanted sex, had thought it was the most important aspect of a relationship. She'd wanted something that'd make her feel like a woman, sexual and strong and satisfied. And she'd got it.

But the bottom line was that he was a soldier. Not just military, in service to his country. But an elite fighting machine, specifically trained and totally focused on dangerous missions. Someone who'd always put country, squad and his career before anyone else in his life.

Men like that were exceptional. Special. And even though she hadn't realized it, that was part of what made Blake so incredible. So maybe she could live with that.

But another part of his job was keeping secrets. She'd never know what he did, where he went. She'd always come second, not just to the mission, but to the classified information that made up eighty percent of his life. By nature, military men kept part of themselves closed off. Private.

That, she couldn't accept.

"Give it a chance, Alexia," Michael said, almost pleading. "At least talk to him."

"Is he paying you?" she asked suspiciously, giving her brother a narrow look.

"I just…" He glanced at his hands, then shrugged and gave her a sad smile. "I just want to see you happy. If you're happy, you'll stick around."

Alexia reached over and squeezed his hand. "I'll stick around anyway, silly."

"No." Michael shook his head. "After all this, you're going to convince yourself that dating Dr. Darling is the right thing to do. Within a year you'll realize how much you hate it, working together will be a nightmare, and you'll quit and move away to escape the misery of it all."

She started to laugh, then realized he was right. That's exactly what she'd do. Wrinkling her nose, Alexia asked, "When'd you get so smart?"

"I've always been smart. You just weren't listening."

"I missed you," Alexia said quietly, reaching out to take his hand. "I don't want to be that far away again. So how about this. You don't push me on dating Blake, and I'll promise not to date Edward. That way you won't drive me crazy, making me wish for what I can't have, and I won't ruin my career and run away."

"If that's the best I can get, I'll take it," her brother said resignedly. "But I still think you should give the Sexy SEAL a chance."

She'd already fallen half in love with him just based on their physical connection. If she gave him a chance—gave them a chance—the rest of the fall would be as easy as breathing.

And she couldn't—wouldn't—let herself fall in love with a man she couldn't communicate with. One who kept part of himself under lock and key.

"I can't," she decided quietly, wishing it didn't hurt so much. They'd known each other less than a week. She shouldn't feel as if someone was tearing part of her heart in two. "Because my prejudices would ruin the relationship in the end anyway."

8

Eight Months Later

"DUDE, YOU'VE TURNED into a total downer."

Cade's words echoed through the empty barracks in Quatar. The rest of the squad was off celebrating their return from Syria. Blake had turned down their invite to join in, wanting to sleep and decompress first.

"Sorry I'm not living up to your entertainment standards," Blake muttered, not bothering to open his eyes.

"You're mooning. Get over her already."

"I'm sleeping. As in resting up after a three-week recon."

Cade's sigh was a work of art. Loud, drawn out and filled with enough exasperation to fuel an obnoxious teenager for a week.

Blake almost smiled. But he still didn't open his eyes. He wanted to sleep. Sleep and work were great. In between the two? Not so great.

Not that he was mooning. That'd be stupid. And Blake didn't waste his time with stupid.

"You need to get over her."

"Over who?"

The silence was glorious.

If only it'd last.

"It's been months. You're so hung up that you barely do anything anymore. Missions, the gym, the dojo, the range. That's your life. You're a cliché, man."

Sad, but true.

Michael had been right. After slamming the door in his face, Alexia hadn't talked to him again. Blake had called. He'd gone by her place. He'd done everything but tattle to her daddy.

Finally, he'd given up.

He wasn't going to waste his time on a woman who couldn't get past her father issues.

"I'm not a cliché. I'm not mooning and I haven't been a monk." There. He'd defended himself against all of Cade's accusations. Maybe now he could get some sleep.

"You're not putting anything into it, either. Sex with random strangers just to relieve the pressure isn't your thing."

"Don't you have a lovelorn column to write?" Blake snapped, sick of thinking about Alexia and totally pissed that Cade wouldn't let it go.

"'Dear Lovelorn LC, I've fallen for the girl I can't have and now can't get over her. How do I heal my broken heart?'"

It might have been funny if it wasn't way too close to the truth.

"Sullivan, you're a pain in my ass."

"Landon!"

Thank God. An interruption Cade couldn't ignore.

"Sir?" Blake sprang to his feet, coming to attention despite the fact that he was off duty, in his boxers and, *seriously,* trying to sleep.

"New orders. Report to the captain."

EYES FOCUSED on the silver eagle gracing the plaque of the United States Navy, Blake stood at attention. The brass behind the desk ignored his presence, multitasking paperwork and a phone call instead.

Shoulders firm, chin high, senses alert, Blake knew his face didn't betray any irritation at waiting, even though it'd been ten minutes already. Nor did any of the questions he had on his mind show in his expression.

He wasn't wondering why he had been pulled from his assignment and ordered back to the Coronado Naval Base without the rest of his team.

Nor was he curious about why this meeting was deemed classified.

Both of those were pretty much Standard Operating Procedure.

The question burning in his gut was why the hell he was reporting directly to Rear Admiral Lane.

Plenty of orders had come down from Lane, but they went through the chain of command. Blake had never had a face-to-face with the rear admiral. He hadn't even seen the guy in person since Admiral Pierce's retirement party last September.

Anger fisted tight in his gut, the same as it always did at the memory of that night.

As he had so many times in the past, he reminded himself that it was stupid to get worked up over a woman he'd barely known. The only reason Alexia was still intriguing was because he hadn't got to spend enough time with her for the shine to wear off. Great sex, a body that haunted his dreams and a personality that had almost convinced him there was such a thing as relationships outside of bed... Nothing to obsess over.

He'd slept with plenty of women in the past few months, enough to wipe away the memory of that wild encounter.

He wasn't a sentimental guy, nor was he the kind who fanatically crushed on some long-forgotten—or supposed-to-be-forgotten—chick.

Nope. No reason to be angry.

No point in remembering the exact texture of her lips, the scent of her hair in the moonlight or the feel of her soft curves pressed into his chest. It was ridiculous to wish he could see her, just one more time, poised naked above him, waiting to ride them both to the heights and depths of passion. The last thing he needed in his life was the distraction of wondering how she was liking her new job, whether she'd adjusted to life in San Diego or if she still missed New York. If she'd unpacked everything and if she'd got to the beach yet this year.

With the same discipline he used to push his body to its limits, to train with the elite and to succeed in missions that most would deem impossible, Blake shoved the memory—and all its accompanying emotional tension—out of his mind.

Better to focus on wondering why the hell he was here.

More for distraction than because he figured he'd find an answer, he started running through a mental list of all the known conflicts that might require a one-man mission.

He hadn't come up with a single idea by the time the rear admiral wound up his phone call.

"Landon," Lane acknowledged when he hung up the receiver.

Already at attention, Blake shifted all of his focus—physical and mental—to his commanding officer.

"Sir."

"You were recently in Syria."

Since it was a statement, not a question, Blake didn't respond. Still staring at the eagle, he was aware his mind raced. The last mission had been a success. The team had even received a thumbs-up from the commander in chief on a job well done. Where was this going?

"In the last year, you've spent six months deployed in the Middle East, completed seventy-two missions and earned yourself three commendations."

That sounded about right. The rear admiral wasn't looking for confirmation, though.

"You have a reputation as a strong team player. A man who understands orders but can think on his feet."

What SEAL didn't?

"You've proven that you're a stickler for the rules of engagement, and will follow them to the letter."

It was all Blake could do not to roll his eyes.

Any guy on the team could be standing here. None of this commentary was unique to Blake's career. So where was the old guy going with it? He wasn't evaluating Blake's service history to fill conversation gaps. It was some kind of test.

One, Blake figured, that he'd already won—or lost, depending on the perspective—given that he was standing here.

But what was at stake?

"While your service record shows an affinity for teamwork and leadership, your C-Sort indicates a leaning toward autonomy and self-reliance. That suggests that you work well alone, possibly even better than you do on a team."

His C-Sort? The admiral had dug all the way back to Blake's initial psych screening for this assignment. What the hell was going on?

For the first time since he'd walked in, Blake stared at the rear admiral. Frowning, he processed the furrow in the older man's brow, the cold sheen in his narrowed eyes.

Whatever was going down, it was big.

"Am I being removed from my team?"

"Temporarily reassigned."

With a quick jerk of his chin, Blake acknowledged the new assignment and waited for further orders. And, hopefully, clarification.

The rear admiral looked out the window for a few seconds, as if sorting through which information he wanted to share. Then, his lips compressed almost white, he met Blake's gaze again. He straightened, hands clasped behind his back, took a deep breath then spoke.

"There's been a kidnapping. A civilian with military ties and potentially dangerous information was forcibly removed from her home two days ago. Operatives have discerned the group behind the act and pinpointed her location."

The words *her* and *military ties* added a layer of urgency to an already volatile mission.

"The cell is based inside the continental United States," the rear admiral informed him. "The leader of this branch of terrorists, as well as a number of those serving him, is a U.S. citizen."

Touchy. And way outside the SEALs' usual M.O.

"In two days' time, a team will neutralize this cell. Every effort will be made to keep the targets alive."

Blake gave a mental grimace. Targets had an unfortunate way of becoming collateral damage. Hostages, even more so.

"Your orders are to extract the hostage. You will go in alone, answering only to me. You will have twenty minutes before the team deploys. You will inform nobody of this assignment, nor will you coordinate with the team itself."

His mind took off in multiple directions. One part wondering why the hell his role in the mission was on blackout. Another part assessing what he'd need to do to pull it off without risking the team's mission or the safety of the hostage. Yet another part was already shifting into mission mode, emotionally distancing himself at the same time he set in place the expectations for victory.

"You were specifically requested for this assignment, Landon."

Blake frowned.

As a SEAL, his training was intense and his skill set diverse. But so was the rest of his team's. He was the Assault Force commander, the radioman and a linguist. And he was damn good at what he did. But, again, so were a lot of the team. So why him, specifically? Blake waited. If Lane wanted him to know who'd put in that request, he'd say so.

The rear admiral shifted. It wasn't the uniform, the rank or the shock of white hair against a rock-hard face that made the man intimidating. It was the cold look of determination that said this was a guy who'd do whatever it took to get the job done, not because he felt the consequences were worthwhile, but because he didn't even see consequences. Only the goal.

After giving Blake another assessing look, he pressed the intercom button on his desk. He didn't say anything though. Just waited.

Blake waited, too. But for less time than it took to exhale. The private door to the right of the rear admiral opened.

His mentor, his recruiter, the man who'd shaped the direction of Blake's career and had fathered the sexiest woman alive, stepped through the door. Pierce didn't say a word. He just stood at ease, his face unreadable as he stared at Blake.

The rear admiral lifted a file from his desk, tapped it a couple of times against his thigh while giving Blake another of those assessing looks. Finally, with a lengthy stare at the admiral, he handed over the file.

"Your assignment." Unspoken was the order that it be read and memorized here in this room. Blake had access to the information, but the contents would stay under lock and key.

Used to that, Blake glanced at the admiral again, but got nothing. Then he unwrapped the cord holding the folder closed and pulled out the stack of papers. On top was an eight-by-ten color photo. His heart stopped. His breath jammed in his throat. A feeling he barely recognized as fear clenched his belly.

His gaze flew to the admiral's.

"Sir?"

Pierce's jaw tightened. His eyes dropped for one second to his hands, then met Blake's again.

"I'm calling in a favor on this. A number of them, actually. I'm sure you understand why."

Shocked, Blake looked at the file again but didn't respond.

Pierce came around the desk in swift, determined strides. He didn't stop until his face was inches from Blake's.

Through gritted teeth, he commanded, "As of this moment, and until the mission is complete, you report directly to me and Rear Admiral Lane. You will rescue her. You will keep her safe."

Cold blue eyes bore into Blake as if imprinting the orders on his brain.

"You bring my daughter back. Safe and sound, Lieutenant."

The *or else* didn't need to be said. The message was implicit in the admiral's furiously set jaw, and in the vicious bite of his words.

"You will rescue her before the team storms the compound. You will get her out, safe and whole. And you will keep her hidden and safe until you get my order to bring her back home."

Blake didn't have to ask if this mission was sanctioned. He knew the rear admiral was dancing on a fine line, doing this favor for his old friend. But he hadn't crossed it. Even if he had…

Blake's gaze dropped to the photo again. Alexia's face stared back at him. An official government ID shot, her brilliant hair was pulled back, but wayward curls escaped to dance happily around her face. The photo captured the brilliant brown of her eyes, the same brown that haunted his dreams. Her smile, with that sexy overbite, was just this side of wicked. He remembered how soft those lips had been under his. How sweet and sexy she'd tasted.

He tried to bank the fury savaging its way through his system. Emotions had no place on a mission. Not a successful one. And this one, he promised himself, would be a success.

He met the admiral's eyes, his own hard with determination.

"I'll bring her back, sir. Safe, sound and secure."

IF SHE COULD JUST KEEP breathing, Alexia promised herself, she'd survive with her life, her sanity and maybe—by some miracle—her faith in humanity.

Eyes closed, carefully inhaling through her teeth to try to block the rancid smell in the room, she focused on calming her mind.

In.

Out.

Just keep breathing in and out.

Don't think about anything but breathing.

"You're going to hyperventilate if you keep sucking in air like that."

Her next breath slid through her teeth with a hiss as she slitted her eyes open to glare at the man across the dining table from her.

The source of the rancid smell, his scent perfectly fit his personality. She'd memorized his features as a part of her promise to herself that she'd not only get out of this nightmare, but that as soon as she did, she'd have as much ammunition as possible to fry his ass.

Short, probably about five-seven, he had that small-man syndrome, flexing his power left and right. Dark hair, brown eyes, a nondescript face marred by a small scar on his chin, he had the beady-eyed look of a rat. Which made sense, since he had the personality of a rabid rodent.

A rabid rodent with a large contingent of creeps on his payroll. The creeps who'd grabbed her on the sidewalk in front of her condo. The creeps who'd put a hood over her head, hauled her to the snowy regions of hell, aka the wilds somewhere in Alaska. The creeps who'd taken turns guarding her when she was locked in her room or the makeshift lab they'd set up. Or, she slanted a look sideways at the big bruiser leaning against the wall of the large dining room, wherever she happened to be. Then there were serving creeps, administrative creeps and, she'd discovered when she'd stood on the back of the chair in her tiny room to peer out the tiny barred window, a tidy number of creeps guarding the perimeter of the icy compound.

"You might as well say something," the rat instructed, his bored tone at odds with the irritated tapping of his glossy fingernail on the arm of his chair. "You're not going back to your cozy room until you detail the progress you made in the lab today."

A seven-by-seven space with no heat, a cot-sans-sheets,

a blanket and a spindle-backed chair and rickety floor lamp didn't quite say cozy to her. But to a rat, maybe that was heaven.

Alexia deliberately took a deep, loud breath in, then exhaled. But she didn't speak.

He tapped louder.

She almost smiled. These tiny rebellions were pointless, but they were all she had. It'd been four days. Four long, nerve-shattering days since she'd been grabbed. Someone had to notice she was gone by now. Michael would have alerted their father. He might not be much in the way of a great parent, but when it came to protecting the interests of the United States and its citizens, he was hell on wheels. Which meant he'd get her out of here soon. At last that's what she'd been promising herself.

For four days.

The first day, exhausted from terror and travel, she'd begged to know why they'd abducted her, pleaded to be released. The rat had said he'd fill her in on what she'd need to do to stay alive in the morning. After she had a nice little rest and time to think about all the possibilities, he'd gloated. Then he'd locked her in that dark, dank *cozy* room.

The second day, fury overshadowing her bone-numbing fear, she'd tried threats as soon as he unlocked her door. The rat had laughed in her face before instructing her to follow him to the dining room. Couldn't have her wasting away from starvation until she was done with her new job.

Since the Science Institute had refused his many legitimate requests, he'd decided it was time to get what he wanted the illegitimate way. Through force and kidnapping. Since she was the public face of the institute's subliminal project, she was clearly—at least in his mind—the expert. It would be her duty, he'd explained over smoked fish, runny eggs and undercooked bacon, to develop a new subliminal program. One that would take the technology she'd been developing for sexual healing and use it to stimulate and heighten anger.

She'd tried to reason with him. The science of true subliminally enhanced emotional response was new, she'd explained. Unlike the cassette tapes of years gone by with their spoken message whispered through soothing music, actually effecting a specific, targeted emotional change via brain waves. Her psychological focus was human sexuality, not anger. She'd never studied how sound related to human perception of negative emotions. She wasn't a neurologist, she didn't know where anger was triggered in the brain, so she couldn't create a program that would target it.

He'd pointed a fork dripping with egg and bacon grease her way and suggested she get her ass to learning before he lost patience. Then he'd had her escorted to what he called her new lab. A room barely bigger than the one she'd slept in, it was fitted with a desk, a workbench and two chairs. A used and slightly beat-up-looking stack of audio and digital equipment littered the bench, including a processor, data streamer and a closed-loop stimulator. Next to that was an array of psych books and a digital tablet.

After ordering her to work, he'd left her there until this morning. With bargain-basement equipment that did her no good, a pile of books that meant nothing, no research access and a ton of time for her brain to scramble between terrified images of what would come next, to blinding hope that someone would get her the hell out of there before she had to face the rat again.

But here she was, pretty much running out of hope.

So she was tuning him out. The games, the threats, the fear. Four years of yoga breathing and tapping into her long-abandoned meditation practice were all she had left. With that in mind, and yes, because she'd seen the irritation on his face, she closed her eyes again and inhaled deeply through her teeth.

"You're doing it wrong," the whiny voice snapped. "You're supposed to inhale through your nose. It's a filter. Are you sure you're a scientist? You don't seem to know very much."

Alexia's eyes popped open, followed quickly by her mouth. Luckily, she saw the gleam in his beady eyes before she spit a word of defense.

She clamped her lips shut.

"I'm not surprised, actually," he mused, contemplating the slab of bloody red steak on his fork. "Disappointed, but after your lack of progress these few days, not surprised at all."

Shifting that same contemplative stare to her face, he wrapped his fat lips around that huge chunk of meat and chewed. A trail of blood dripped down the side of his mouth, over his receding chin, then plopped on the front of his white shirt. He didn't seem to notice.

He was waiting for her to rise to the bait.

Alexia refused.

His eyes gleamed, as if the more defiance she showed, the happier he was.

"I'd have thought a woman like yourself, with all those fancy degrees and who's made a show of thumbing her nose at her family, would be a little smarter."

Alexia's blood froze. She'd figured this was all about her research. But if he knew who her family was, that changed things. Was this really about creating an anger switch? Or did it have something to do with her father? If the latter, why the elaborate charade?

"Please," she said, trying to sound reasonable and calm instead of freaked out and frenzied. "Just let me go. I can't do what you're asking. You're smart enough to have researched the technology yourself. You know the equipment you have here isn't adequate. The research isn't cohesive enough to work with."

Yes, she was playing fast and loose with the terms *smart* and *research* there. But she figured saving her life was a good enough excuse to employ a few lies and fake flattery.

"You're on the verge of a breakthrough. You just did an interview on TV last month. It's in the papers, other scientists are commenting on it in their blogs," he said, shaking his finger at her as if she had done something naughty.

Blogs? Seriously? Alexia's nerves stretched tight, ravaged from alternately fearing for her life and peering into corners looking for the hidden cameras that would prove this was all some elaborate, sick hoax.

"So there's no reason you can't take the same research and give it a little twist. Passion is just as easily channeled into anger as it is into something as trivial as sex."

"I told you, it's not a simple matter of flipping a switch. My research has been focused on the physical body and healing. Not on the emotions. I don't know how to tap into anger, fury or any of the other destructive emotions you want."

His contemplative stare didn't change. He didn't even blink. Maybe he was more snake than rat.

"Perhaps you just need a little motivation," he decided. That damn finger still tapping, he tilted his head to one side as he gave her body a thorough inspection. Her skin crawled as if someone had just dipped her in a vat of lice.

"You're a pretty woman. Robert—" he indicated the henchman who most often guarded Alexia "—has expressed an interest in your charms. Perhaps I should reward his exemplary service, hmm?"

Her eyes blurry with fear, Alexia's gaze slid to the henchman, whose own beady eyes were gleaming with lust. Bile rose in her throat, but she was too paralyzed with terror to even throw up.

"Of course, Robert did go a little far with his last reward," the rat continued in that same contemplative tone. "She was useless to us when he was through. It's hard to see much through the snowstorm, but if you look out your window, you can see her grave just on the other side of the electric fence."

Black dots danced in front of Alexia's eyes, her breathing so shallow she didn't think any oxygen was reaching her brain.

"I'm more inclined to wait on the reward," he said slowly, pausing to sip his wine, giving her time to take a small step back from the panicked cliff she'd been about to dive over. "Myself, I find rape a poor persuasion. If the mind is broken, the body isn't good for much except more of the same. And I need your mind in good working order."

Alexia wasn't sure if her mind would ever work again, even as it shied away from the hideous images she couldn't stop from running through it.

"So many possibilities to consider," he mused, now tapping his lower lip as if that would help him decide. "I'll have to sleep on it and let you know in the morning."

His smile slid into a smirk. "In the meantime, I suggest you trot on over to the lab and see what you can do now that you're a little more motivated."

"You can't do this," she breathed, half denial, half prayer.

"I can do anything I want," he said with a dismissive wave of his hand. "Go. Robert will see you to the lab."

Alexia got to her feet, subtly resting her fingertips on the edge of the table until her knees stopped shaking enough to support her.

"Go on," the rat ordered, flicking his fingers toward the door. "Get to work."

Yeah, she decided, trying to find the fury through the choking waves of fear threatening to overwhelm her.

He was definitely a snake.

9

FOURTEEN HOURS LATER, Alexia finally understood what it was to have fear leach every ounce of energy from a body.

She was completely numb.

She cradled her head in her arms and tried to stop her teeth from chattering.

From her bare toes—made colder every time she glanced at the window to see the white blizzard of snow swirling outside—to the top of her aching head, she was ice.

Desperate for a focal point other than the hideous visions her captor had stuck in her head, she had resorted to digging into the books. Somewhere around hour three, she had filled a notebook. Not anything that'd produce the results he wanted. But maybe enough to make it look as if she could, which might buy her some time.

The words were a blur on the page now.

It took Alexia a minute to realize that was because she was crying, her tears making the ink run.

A sound, barely a whisper of the wind, caught her attention. Her body braced. Tension, so tight even her hair hurt, gripped her. Barely daring to breathe, she shifted her head just a bit in her cradling arms so she could peek over her shoulder.

Crap.

She blinked, trying to focus on the figure standing inside a window that should be too tiny for a body to fit through. The freezing air wrapped around her like a shroud, making her blink again.

Her shivers turned to body-racking shakes. Alexia still didn't bother raising her head.

"I sure wish hallucinations came with temperature control," she muttered to her biceps.

The figure moved. She blinked a couple of times, waiting for it to fade. But it came closer.

And closer.

The closer it came, the more sure she was that this was pure fantasy, woven by a generous mind eager to give her a sweet escape.

"Let's go," the fantasy ordered. She wasn't surprised it sounded like Blake. All her fantasies revolved around the sexy SEAL. Most were naked, though, and the only shivers involved were sexually inspired.

"Sure, I'll go with you," she bartered in a teasing tone. Might as well humor her mind, since it'd gone to all this trouble of creating her dream man. "But if I do, you have to reward me with kisses and sexual delights. I've done the calculations. By showing up at the party and outing yourself as forbidden fruit," she informed the hallucination, "you deprived me of at least twenty-seven orgasms. I figured that's how many I'd have gotten before the heat ran its course."

The figure froze for a second, then he shook his head as if clearing his ears of static.

He looked like a walking arsenal, with an automatic weapon slung across his shoulder, pistols at both hips and a slew of scary-looking devices on his utility belt. He wore a white snow-camo jacket and hood with a cloth mask covering the lower half of his face. All she could see were his eyes. They were the same vivid blue she remembered, then they grew distant again. Assessing, constantly shifting around the room, and almost as cold as the snow outside.

"Twenty-seven, hmm?" He stepped over to the door, his moves slick and silent. He pressed an ear against the wall, checked some gadget in his hand, then gave her a commanding wave of his hand as if ordering her to stand.

"Tell you what, let's get the hell out of here, and then we can talk about payback on those orgasms."

"Payback is double," she decided then and there. Why not. It was her fantasy after all.

For a brief second, she saw amusement flash in those bright eyes. For that instant, she felt the same connection that'd zinged between her and the real Blake Landon almost a year ago. Her heart sang with joy, so sure it'd found its perfect match.

Silly heart.

Then he shifted, shrugging a pack off his back. He dug into it, pulling out things even more tempting than fifty-four screaming orgasms.

Warm clothes. Thick socks, heavy boots and a coat.

She moaned. A heavy coat, with a furry hood.

This fantasy just kept getting better and better.

A cold wind whipped through the room. Ice showered her back and freezing snowflakes flecked her hair and face.

Slowly, terrified if she moved too fast he'd disappear, Alexia raised her head off her arms.

He was still there.

She blinked.

He held out the socks and boots.

Wetting her lips, she hesitated. Then, having to know one way or the other, she reached out. The wool socks were like fire, hot and welcoming.

The boots waggled. Her gaze flew from the sturdy cold-weather footwear to the man's face. He was real? He was here to rescue her?

Alexia's mind couldn't seem to take it in.

Thankfully, though, her body was all over the idea, grabbing the socks and yanking them over her frozen toes.

"You're real?" she whispered, reaching out for the boots.

"As real as you are, sweetheart. Let's get our asses in gear. We have five minutes before this place is blown to hell."

She should be scared, shouldn't she?

Or relieved?

Excited or ecstatic or grateful.

Maybe the weather had frozen her emotions, too, because she couldn't feel a thing.

Except the cold.

Like moving through a dream, Alexia snuggled herself into the warmth of the white camouflage winter gear. Her brain was foggy as she tried to accept that Blake was real. The possibility that he was a figment of her desperate imagination didn't stop her from following him to the window, though.

Her movements were stiff as she took his hand to help her climb onto the chair, wishing she could feel him through their thick gloves, her body feeling as if she'd just recovered from a vile flu.

He was real.

He was here.

She was rescued.

"Is there a team outside?" she asked. As much as she wanted out of this room, she knew there was an arsenal pointed at the window, armed guards who'd be thrilled to use her for target practice and a seriously strong chance that she'd break a leg crawling out a second-story window.

"We're on our own," he said quietly, stepping up to the window, too, and using his infrared binoculars to check the landscape. "There's a rope hanging just outside the ledge. Do you see it?"

"On our own?"

How was that possible? SEALs operated in teams.

Suddenly her brain sparked to life. Like a limb waking, the tingles were painful as she tried to figure out what was going on.

"Where's the rest of the team? Your backup?" It was unfortunate that her words came out shrill with an overtone of hysteria. But, well, she was pretty close to hysterical, so it was only to be expected.

"We're the team, you and I. We're not going to need backup because nobody's going to be paying us any attention in—" he glanced at his watch again "—four minutes."

He wasn't hysterical. She frowned, peering at his face to try to see if his mellow certainty was an act or if he was really okay with being a one-man rescue show.

The more she looked, the calmer she became. As if she was absorbing his confidence and strength. Granted, he was almost completely shrouded in warm winter gear. But his voice, his stance, his entire persona were one hundred percent assured. He was trained for this, she told herself. He'd done hundreds, maybe thousands, of missions in much riskier situations. He'd served during wartime, for crying out loud.

But that was him.

She was pretty much a wimp.

"We're really on our own?" she whispered. Then, with

a shaky breath, she glanced at the rickety desk and sad stool. Maybe she should stay here.

"Do you trust me?"

Her gaze flew to his face. Covered in goggles, surrounded by a cinched hood, she could barely make out his features.

"Do you trust me?" he repeated.

Her heart sighed, even as terror clutched her guts. They'd have to sneak through a terrorist encampment filled with gleeful murderers to hide in a vicious snowstorm. Just the two of them, with no backup. No access to help. Nobody to rescue them if something went wrong.

Of course, if they stayed here, they'd be blown to bits in four minutes.

Alexia wet her parched lips, then nodded.

"I trust you."

Blake moved closer. He took her right hand, so warm now inside its heated glove, and tucked it up inside the wristband of her coat. Then he did the same with the left.

Alexia's body came awake much faster than her mind had. Warmth, not felt since the last time he touched her, slid through her body. Like liquid pleasure, it permeated, slowly trickling all the way to her toes.

He tugged on the zipper of her coat, snugging it up to just below her throat, then with hands so gentle she almost wept, he smoothed her hair away from her face and lifted the hood of the coat. The fabric was so thick, so warm. When he pulled the strings closed to cinch it tight around her face, she felt as if she was in a sound tunnel, the beat of her heart amplified in her ears.

He let go for just a second to reach into the pack and pull out a pair of goggle-like glasses, sliding them onto her nose. Then he tugged the zipper higher, snapping the front of the jacket tight so not a whisper of cold air could touch anything but the little bits of her face still exposed.

Alexia wasn't sure she'd ever felt so protected. So cared for.

"Do whatever I tell you," he said softly, his gaze intense as he stared into her eyes. "Stay low, follow in my exact steps. I'll get you home safe and sound. I promise."

Unable to believe otherwise when he was looking at her like this, she nodded.

"I need you to really trust me, Alexia. Not because I'm the lesser of two evils, but because you have complete faith that I'll keep you safe. That I know exactly what I'm doing, that I'm damn good at it and that you know without a doubt that I'm going to get you out of here."

The huge lump in her throat made it hard to swallow, so Alexia just nodded instead of speaking.

"You're sure?"

She took a deep breath, then swallowed again. "I trust you, completely," she promised breathlessly.

His smile was like the rising sun. Warm, vivid and beautiful. She melted. Then, his hands still on the zipper of her jacket, he tugged her closer. Bent his head and kissed her.

Oh, baby.

His lips were as soft, as delicious, as magical as she'd remembered. The kiss was short, way too short, but so sweet she would have cried if she wasn't afraid the tears would freeze on her face.

He slowly pulled back, his eyes still locked on hers. Then he flicked a button in the side of the goggles, activating a buzzing in her ears. Communication device, she realized.

"What's that for?" she whispered, her breath an icy mist between them. "Luck?"

"I don't need luck, sweetheart. I'm the best. That's why I was handpicked to rescue you. That—" he kissed her again, just a quick brush of his chilly lips against hers "—that was because I've missed you."

Nothing like fogging a woman's brain and sending her heart into a nosedive of delight to get her to climb out a tiny window into an enemy-filled snow-hell.

She didn't know if she should admit she'd missed him or not. If she did, it'd be like a deathbed confession, said because she knew she'd never have another chance. Call her superstitious, but she'd rather wait to make any emotional declarations until they were safe.

"Lucky me," she said instead, putting all the things she couldn't say into her smile and hoping he understood. "I'm glad I rate the best."

BLAKE WISHED she hadn't smiled.

It touched something inside him, ratcheted the stakes so much higher.

He was here to do a job, and he couldn't do that job if he let emotions in. Any kind of emotions. The key to a successful mission was a clear mind, the ability to think three steps ahead and a solid handle on the outcome, while keeping a fluid sense of the steps in between.

He'd learned early in his career that the only way to succeed was to shut out fear. Worrying, in any form, was the equivalent of strapping a bull's-eye on his back.

He shouldn't have kissed her.

He was on a mission.

She was his mission.

Kissing the rescue target was totally against protocol.

He hadn't been able to resist.

Blake hefted his pack onto his shoulders again, then checked the time.

Two minutes.

"Let's go."

He made sure she was situated on the chair, then grabbed the windowsill and pulled himself up. He glanced at her again.

"Promise. You do exactly what I say."

"Promise."

"Even if I say run, without me, you'll do it. The coordinates, a compass and a GPS are in your jacket. Don't take it off."

Her eyes were huge behind the protective lenses. Her nod was a jerk of her chin. But her lips were pressed in a determined line, and if her hands were shaking inside her gloves, the tremor was mild.

She'd hold up.

Blake glanced at the compound again, then reached down to pull the cloth, embedded with a tiny communication wire, across her lower face. Then he did the same to his own.

"Ready?" he whispered.

She gave a tiny start, indicating that she'd heard him through her headphones, and nodded again.

"Then let's rock."

He flipped the switch on his lenses, triggering the heat sensors. Two guards on the east side, one on the west. He glanced at his watch.

One minute.

One hand holding his weapon, Blake shimmied through the window, gripping the stones surrounding it and pulling himself free. He reached in to aid Alexia, but she'd already grabbed ahold of the sill and had herself halfway out. He took her hand, pulling her up so her toes were balanced on the sill and the rest of her against the stone wall, then bent low to snag the rope.

"Wait until I'm down, then follow," he said quietly.

Her gaze ricocheted around the compound as if she was watching for the devil to come riding in. But she nodded. Using the rope, his back to the wall so he could watch for threats, he quickly lowered himself to the ground. He sank into the snow to midcalf.

It only took him a second to reach into the small white pack he'd stashed at the base of the wall and pull out the snowshoes. Fully alert, his finger still on the trigger of his revolver, he swiftly stepped into them.

"Go," he told Alexia.

She flew down the wall. He winced twice as her body bounced off the stones, but she didn't slow. Clearly she wanted the hell out of here.

He liked giving a lady what she wanted.

"Put these on," he told her as soon as she'd released the rope. She squinted at the snowshoes, then nodded. He made sure she knew what she was doing as she put the first one on. He glanced at his watch as she finished the second.

One minute past. The explosion should have already happened, providing cover for their escape. He scanned the guards again. Still in place.

Recalling one of Phil's favorite sayings, *no worries, no bull's-eyes,* he reached into his boot and pulled out his backup Glock.

"Ready?" he asked Alexia, giving her a once-over.

"Ready."

He handed her the gun.

Her gasp echoed in his ears. But she took it. With a sureness that'd do the admiral proud, she checked the clip, the safety. Her breath just as loud in his speaker again, she nodded.

What a woman.

Grinning behind his mask, Blake tilted his head to the north. Time to go.

As soon as he stepped a foot from the building, he was buffeted by driving snow.

"Hold on to my belt," he instructed.

A second later he felt the pressure of her fingers. Good. Now he could focus ahead without needing to check her progress.

Without the wind and snow, they could have made the hundred and fifty yards to the fence line in less than half a minute. But running at a crouch through a foot of snow took twice that.

When they reached the bare expanse of wire fence, he stooped. Alexia did the same. Watching constantly, he pulled out what looked like a pair of tiny rubber pincers. He'd come in overhead, rappelling from the trees to the top of the building. To leave, they needed to cut the barbed wire.

He hesitated. As soon as he clamped the wires, an alarm would sound. If the compound had already been hit, the chaos would have covered their escape.

This, or the gates, were the only way out. Orders were to stay covert and not to engage the enemy.

So they'd stick with the plan. And run a little faster.

He took a deep breath.

Then, knowing what was likely to come, he looked at Alexia. Her brown eyes were huge, her lips white. Still, she gave him a reassuring smile.

"So far so good," she whispered.

He nodded.

"As soon as I cut this, we're tagged. There's a vehicle waiting a mile to the east. In it is a radio in case you have to communicate with anyone." He hesitated, then decided she was strong enough—had to be strong enough—to face reality. "If we're engaged, you keep running. Don't wait for me. Don't look back or try to help. Head for the vehicle, get the hell out of here."

"But—"

"Get the hell out," he repeated firmly.

Her chin trembled. He watched, fascinated, as she breathed in, seeming to suck strength from the air. She squared her jaw, resolve steely in her eyes. And she nodded.

"Attagirl," he whispered.

Then he clamped the wires.

The world exploded. Fire filled the air. Rocks flew. The ground shook. Alexia ducked low, covering the back of her head with her hands.

"And there's the cavalry," he said with a grin, cutting the wires. "Go."

She gave a wide-eyed look at the now-flaming building, bodies scurrying like rats to and from the inferno. Then she crouched down low, sliding through the wires he'd cut.

"Hold my belt and keep up," he told her as soon as they were clear. "Most of the enemy will be focused on the invasion. But if they're smart, they'll have people securing the perimeter."

"They didn't impress me as being too smart," she said, showing a little of that sass he remembered so fondly. "But they did have the devil's own luck on their side. So run as fast as you want. I'll keep up."

The rapid-fire pinging of automatic weapons got louder. The team had engaged, he noted. And since they had no idea he or Alexia were here, they'd be taken as the enemy if spotted.

"Let's go."

Taking her at her word, he set off at a low, crouching sprint. Moving through the snow, both the thick ground cover and the flurries buffeting them backward, was hardly fast. But—he checked his GPS to make sure they were on track—they were making progress.

"Hold," he ordered. He stopped, still hunkered down, and scanned the area for signs of body heat. Nothing.

"Okay, let's go."

"Go? Where? How?"

"Vehicle," he said, gesturing to what looked like one of the many snowdrifts in the blurry white landscape. When she shook her head in confusion, he pushed through the snow—hip deep here—and unerringly found the loose end of the white tarp. With a tug, he uncovered the snowmobile he'd stashed.

"This is a vehicle?" She gaped. "Are you sure?"

He grinned, swinging one leg over the seat. "Climb on."

Giving him, then the snowmobile, a doubtful look, she shook her head before climbing on behind him. There wasn't much sexy about the half foot of fabric between their bodies, but Blake's blood still hummed when her thighs clamped tight against his hips. Her arms wrapped around his waist, holding tight to his jacket. As soon as she felt settled, he pressed the ignition and, with one last glance at the flaming sky to the west of the trees, took off.

They flew across the snow, flurries pounding against them as if protesting their escape. He watched his GPS, double-checking the few landmarks along the way to make sure they were on track.

Twenty minutes later, after taking a couple side trips and doubling back to make sure they weren't followed, they reached the side of a mountain. He cut the snowmobile's engine and, muscles trembling from the exertion of holding the vehicle steady in the intense winds, looked around. The helicopter would pick them up on top. At the base, camouflaged by icy brush and snow, was a domed tent. He didn't see any new tracks in or out, but wasn't taking any chances.

"I'm going to make sure it's secure. You move forward and take the controls."

He dismounted, waiting for her to grip the handlebars. As soon as she did, he pulled out his infrared binoculars again and checked the perimeter. Five minutes later, but never losing her from sight, he returned to the snowmobile. Alexia hadn't moved. He could tell because she had at least three inches of snow on her now.

"All clear," he told her.

Her eyes were huge behind the plastic lenses, swimming with exhaustion, fear and relief. She didn't move, though.

"Ready to get out of the snow?"

Her nod was more along the lines of a shiver.

Knowing he needed to get her to warmth quickly, Blake opted for the fastest route. He reached out and lifted her into his arms. She didn't make a sound. She did, however, wrap her hands around him and hold tight.

He liked how it felt, even through the miles of insulated fabric between them.

When he reached the tent, he shifted her, but didn't let go. He tugged open the Velcro closure, then unzipped the canvas. It wasn't until they were inside, lamp on and flap secured again, that he put her gently on her feet.

He waited until she'd stopped swaying, then unhooked the scarf from his hood and grinned.

"Welcome to your temporary home sweet home."

10

ALEXIA'S HEAD WAS SPINNING. She wasn't so sure her body wasn't, too.

The last five days had been surreal. Like something out of a horrible nightmare that not even her own subconscious would torture her with. And now it was over?

Or, she blinked and looked around the tent, almost over?

The tent was awfully well equipped for a temporary stop. Two cots, a cookstove, an array of equipment that looked as if it could control rocket ships. A small arsenal in one corner and a table and chairs in the other. And Blake in the center. Boxes were piled at the back wall and, she squinted, there was a stack of books on one of the cots.

As always, her gaze landed on Blake.

Nerves that'd gone numb on the bone-bruising flight over the snow started coming to life again with big, snapping bites.

He wasn't paying any attention, though. He'd pushed back his hood and now set his goggles aside so he could pull on a radio headset.

She watched carefully, noting what buttons he pushed, which switches he flipped.

"Base, this is Boy Scout. Hostage secured. Will await your go. Boy Scout out."

"That's it?" she asked, frowning as he turned everything off with a push of his finger. She wanted to grab the radio and yell into it. To insist someone hurry the hell up and come to get them. She wanted to go home, dammit.

"That's it," he said.

No, she wanted to moan. She wanted a shower and warm clothes. A bowlful of hot fudge. Her own bed, popcorn, to hug her brother.

"Where are we?" she whispered, more than ready to hear him say the icy bowels of hell.

"Alaska. North Slope," he told her as he moved around the perimeter of the tent, turning on small heaters so the space was soon a warm cocoon. Then he flipped on a series of tiny monitors. At first they all looked white, as though they weren't tuned in. Alexia stepped closer, her eyes narrowed as she realized the white was snow. Then she saw the angled rock he'd parked the snowmobile behind.

Security cameras.

Did he really think someone might follow them? That, and a million more questions chased through her mind. But the first ones to tumble out were, "How long are we waiting here? Is someone picking us up? Who sent you to get me?"

"We're here until we're told otherwise," was the only answer he gave.

"Is that going to be hours? A day? Two? What's that mean?" Alexia realized her voice had hit a pitch high enough to trigger an avalanche, but she couldn't help herself. Feeling trapped, barely able to breathe, she yanked the kerchief from her face and ripped at the strings tying her hood closed. Her fingers, clumsy and fat in the thick gloves, couldn't undo it.

Her breath was coming in gasps now. Black spots sped across her vision, racing one another from side to side. Before she could give in to the scream building in her throat, Blake was there.

His knuckles were warm as they brushed her frozen face, fingers making swift work of the ties, before he gently pushed the hood back and pulled the goggles off.

"Breathe," he instructed quietly. "Pull the air into your belly. Attagirl. Hold it, then let it out."

Her eyes locked on his, she followed his breath, listened to his instructions, and slowly, painfully reeled in the fragile threads of her control.

"Sorry," she murmured as she started to feel like herself again. The heat warming her cheeks should have been welcome in this bitter cold, but shame was never comfortable.

"Nothing to be sorry about," he told her as he continued to gently release her from the coat's bindings, then slipped the gloves off her hands. If he tried to take her boots and socks, she just might have to smack him. It'd be a long time before she wanted to be barefoot again, she realized. "You're exhausted, stressed and probably starving. The natural expectation after being rescued is to go home."

"Can you tell me why I can't?" she asked in a low whisper, not taking her eyes off his. She waited for him to prevaricate or outright refuse. That's what her father would do. All information—right down to which state they'd be attending school in the following month—had always been imparted on a need-to-know basis.

"This is a two-stage mission," he explained. "Rescuing you is stage one. Neutralizing the enemy is stage two. If we're pulled out, it could compromise the team's efforts.

Added to that, it's nighttime. It's safer to wait until light to head out again."

Alexia's jaw dropped.

"What?" he asked, pausing in the act of taking off his own jacket and hanging it with hers on a hook.

"You, well… You answered my question." She realized how stupid it sounded when she said the words. But she'd never gotten answers as a kid. Had been told time and again that good little soldiers followed orders without question—that questioning was a sign of disrespect, of showing doubt toward one's superior.

"You didn't ask for classified information," Blake said, dismissing what she thought of as a miracle with a laugh. "I'll answer whatever I can. You have the right to know what's going on."

It was as if he'd twisted a spigot. Before she realized it was happening, Alexia's cheeks were wet with tears. Her breath came in hiccupping gasps as she fell apart.

He looked at her as if she'd just turned into an alien giraffe with four heads and an Uzi pointed at his man parts. Horrified, shocked and desperate to make it stop.

"I'm sorry," she wailed, trying to control her sobs.

"What…" He shook his head, clearly realizing that this wasn't the time for a reasonable discussion. Then he crossed the tent and pulled her into his arms.

She didn't care that she'd spent months being angry with him, or that she'd imagined countless scenarios in which he saw her again and, miserable and unable to get his party on *sexually* without her, he'd begged her to let him into her life again.

In her imagination, she'd always turned him away.

In real life, she grabbed on as if he was the only oxygen in the room. As soon as she did, her tears slowed. Her heart stopped aching. She felt like a scared little girl and he was her security blanket. Now she wanted to wrap him all around her.

"I don't know what's wrong," she said, her words as shaky as her breath. "I'm safe, right? I'm away from that lunatic and his insane demands. He can't hurt me. His henchman can't touch me, right?"

Blake's arms stiffened around her, his fingers digging into her spine as he pulled her closer, tighter. As if he could wrap himself around her as a shield, keeping her safe. Protected.

"You're safe with me," he vowed.

She never wanted to be anywhere else.

Realizing she'd plummeted into dangerous thinking, Alexia drew in a little more of his calm, got her thoughts and her breathing under control, then slowly pulled back.

"Thank you," she said, wrinkling her nose in embarrassment. "I'm sorry to cry all over you. I guess SEALs really are trained to handle any emergency."

His eyes narrowed, as if he knew she'd tossed his job out to put a wedge between them. He didn't call her on it, though. Maybe he liked the wedge? Alexia frowned, then rubbed her damp cheeks dry.

"I don't suppose you have a hairbrush, or something I can use to wash my face," she asked. "Or, you know, a hairdresser and manicurist stashed in one of those packs."

"There," he said, pointing to the bunk on the left. On it were two packs, one smaller, one larger. "Clothes, toiletries, whatnot. Over there is a makeshift bathroom. No bathing facilities, but you can change."

Alexia followed his gestures, then looked back at him and wet her lips. Get naked, with just a flimsy piece of fabric separating them? Her body trembled at the idea, wanting desperately to beg him to get naked with her. But that wasn't going to happen, she warned her body. He was off-limits. Totally wrong for her, and she wasn't stupid enough to make the same mistake twice.

"Thank you," she murmured, lifting the pack and digging in to find not only a hairbrush and toothbrush, but ponytail holders, thick wool leggings, thermal underwear and a sweater. She wanted to ask who his personal shopper was, but figured the less said to bring attention to the fact that she was about to get naked, the better.

"I'll get dinner ready while you change," he told her.

Alexia narrowed her eyes. He didn't sound as if he cared that she was going to strip down. Not excited, not intrigued. Nothing.

Fine. It wasn't as though she wanted him to want to see her naked. She'd ended that part between them and for a damn good reason.

When Alexia realized that it was taking all her control not to add *so there* and stick out her tongue, she sighed. Clearly, the ordeal was messing with her way too much.

It might have been residual irritation, or probably nerves that she'd give in to her body's urgings and call out for him, but Alexia changed in record time. She didn't want to touch the nasty, five-days-worn clothes once she'd stripped them off, but it wasn't as if the tent came with maid service. So she bundled them up and, noticing a couple of small plastic bags tied to a rope, stuffed them into one. There. Trash.

She used the canteen water to brush her teeth and wash her face, then spent a luxuriously long time running the brush through her tangled mass of hair.

Once it was pulled into a tidy French braid and she felt clean and warm and real again, she pulled back the curtain and rejoined Blake.

Why, oh why did she have to have values? He looked so deliciously sexy standing there in winter camo fatigues tucked into his boots and a long-sleeved white T-shirt. She tried reminding herself that the silver chain she could see along the back of his neck belonged to his dog tags. Making him a soldier boy. *Off-limits, Alexia,* she wanted to yell. But her body didn't care. All it could see was how great he looked.

"Hungry?" he said, giving her a friendly-yet-distant look over his shoulder.

Clearly, he had no problem forgetting about the two days of constant, mind-blowing sex they'd shared. She sniffed. Either that or they hadn't blown his mind enough for him to see her as anything but a mission objective.

And that kiss. She forced herself not to sigh and melt at the memory, since she now knew it was probably just his way of reassuring her. Keeping her from getting hysterical. Or, who knew, maybe luck, as she'd first said.

Before she could pout too much, her stomach—the only part of her body not craving Blake's touch—growled.

"Hungry it is," he said, grinning and setting two plates, steam rising temptingly, on the table.

Alexia placed the pack on her designated cot and joined him.

"Field rations?" she guessed with a grimace. "My father used to insist we have them for dinner once a month. It was supposed to make us appreciate what soldiers had to deal with while protecting our way of life."

"Did it?"

"No," she remembered, wrinkling her nose. "But it did solidify my determination not to serve in the military."

Blake's grin warmed her more than all the space heaters combined. That feeling—and starvation—got her through the first few bites. Then the flavor hit her taste buds.

She poked into the open food box he'd set between them until she found salt. It took two packets before she could get through the other half of her meal. She glanced at Blake, who was spooning up his as if it was covered in chocolate.

"You don't actually like this—" she was hesitant to call it food "—stuff, do you?"

He shrugged, still scooping up the tan goo. "It's not that bad. Growing up, I was mostly hungry, so I tend to focus more on filling my belly than the taste threshold."

She wanted to ask why he'd been hungry. What his up-bringing had been like. Was that a part of why he'd joined the military? For three square meals—or the equivalent? She wrinkled her nose at the mushy stuff on her plate. Did he have siblings? A family? Were they still hungry or had they found their way?

A million questions raced through her mind, but she couldn't ask any of them. She felt it was private, that she had no right to poke or prod. She'd been fine with the right to lick her way down his body and to do a naked dance on his face, but ask personal questions? Totally taboo.

Which was ridiculous. So was the fact that while she'd claimed to want communication with him in the past, she'd never wondered any of those things. She'd only focused on the parts of his life that she thought impacted her. And then, when she'd found out just how strong that impact was, she'd slammed the door shut.

She poked her spoon into the stew again, trying to control the urge to cry. Again. God, she was a mess.

"If you eat all your dinner, I have chocolate for dessert," Blake said in a singsong voice.

Her eyes flew to his face.

"Chocolate?"

"Yep. Chocolate bars, chocolate powder, chocolate syrup."

"Noooo," she breathed in a reverent moan.

"Yep."

She looked around the tent, wondering where he'd hidden it. She hadn't seen any in the box of gross dinner choices. Then, because chocolate made everything more appetizing, she dived into the stew, eating it fast enough that she didn't have to taste it.

"There," she said three minutes later, holding out her cleaned plate. "Chocolate time."

"You're done already?" Surprise clear in his blue eyes, Blake laughed. But he took her plate, put it in a bag, then pulled a small knapsack from beneath one of the bunks.

"It's all yours."

Her fingers trembled, not a new thing for her this week. But this time it was excitement shivering through them as she undid the buckles.

"Yum," she moaned again when she saw the stash inside. At least two-dozen chocolate bars, three cans of familiar brown syrup and a large pouch with two sections, one with brown powder and the other with white. Chocolate milk to go, just add water?

Her fingers had already wrapped around a candy bar when she realized this was a lot of soothing sweetness. Enough to last awhile. A long while.

She bit her lip.

"Should I be rationing it?" she asked Blake quietly.

He paused in the act of emptying another pouch onto his plate and met her eyes. His gaze shifted to the radio, then scanned the monitors before meeting hers again.

"Just enough so that you don't make yourself sick," he said.

Alexia still hesitated.

"We're waiting until we get word that the compound is secured and the team has neutralized everyone inside," he told her, his voice so quiet and matter-of-fact that it took her a second to realize he was filling her in on the mission objective. "As soon as they give the all-clear, someone will contact us with pickup coordinates. How long that takes simply depends on the level of resistance the team meets back there."

"The guy was crazy," she said, carefully pulling a single candy bar from the knapsack, then deliberately closing the flap. "He talked about starting a war, about the loyalty of his troops. There were too many there for me to count."

"Numbers don't matter. Strategy is what counts. And SEALs rock the strategy."

"I've heard that rumor," she said with a smile. "Is this your usual job? Hostage hand-holding?"

His lips twitched. He crossed the tent and stopped in front of her.

"What are you doing?"

Alexia held her breath as excitement swirled in her belly. Personal prejudices being what they were, she'd never been turned on by a guy in uniform, or in camo or even wearing dog tags and low-riding jeans. Soldiers were totally not her thing.

Except Blake.

She was horribly afraid that if she wasn't careful, he'd become her *every*thing.

He reached out and took her hand in his. His fingers entwined with hers, then he gave them a gentle shake.

"Holding hands."

BLAKE LOVED THE WAY she laughed. The sound of it, rich and husky. The way it made her dark eyes dance with delight. The look of her face, all lit up and happy.

He loved the feel of her fingers, slender and warm in his. Relief so intense it made him want to drop to his knees poured through him. She was here. He'd got her out alive, safe and sound.

He couldn't claim he'd never been worried on a mission. Since Phil's death, worry was a second skin, always looming, never comfortable. But scared? He'd never understood real fear until he'd opened that file and realized Alexia was his target. He'd used the fear, iced it down and applied it to fuel his moves, to make sure he was hyper-vigilant. To get Alexia to safety.

They weren't quite there yet. But at the sight of her smile, watching her come back to life as the terror started to fade, he was filled with so many emotions he'd never felt before. It made him wish for things he'd never thought of. Made him care, way too much. Cade had accused him of mooning over Alexia. Blake realized now he'd just been waiting.

And if he'd had the words, if he had a clue what to say, he'd have made some big emotional declaration.

His gut clenched, the hair on the back of his neck standing on end.

He owed his life to those warning signals, so he automatically stopped, mentally gauging the danger.

Alexia, he realized.

She wasn't a threat to his physical safety.

She was a threat to his way of life.

If he let these emotions grow, he'd give in to anything she asked. Like leaving the military. Giving up his career. Growing out his hair. Hell, he was pretty sure he'd even get one of those dogs women carried in their purses if she asked.

Slowly, trying not to make a show of it and get her upset again, he released her hand.

He'd rather have the fear back.

Or at least that nice safe distance time and her anger had provided. Because now that she was here, right here in front of him again? With all these crazy thoughts and emotions going on? She was a bigger danger than the wannabe terrorist and his cadre of idiots back there.

"I guess hand-holding really is a part of your job description," she said, her laugh a little stiff. He wondered if she'd been hit with emotional overload, too. He doubted it. She'd already faced the threat of her life's destruction. Flicking him off again probably didn't even register.

Good. He just had to keep it that way. Make sure his position as a SEAL, his connection with her father, stayed clear in her mind.

That'd keep her hands off him.

And hopefully he had enough training and self-discipline to keep his own off her.

Before he could dismiss the hand-holding as a nothing gesture, or figure out a way to bring her dad into the conversation, the radio light flashed, a low buzz indicating a message was coming in.

Saved by an unexpected communiqué. Not wanting to alarm Alexia, he kept his smile in place.

"Well, hand-holding and answering the phone. Or radio, in this case," he said, walking over to see what was there.

His expression didn't change as he read the intel.

The compound belonged to one Hector Lukoski. The son of a known terrorist with Syrian ties, Lukoski was trying to make a name for himself apart from his father. Well trained in defensive measures, he had an underground hideout. The team had confirmed that there was only one way in or out, and had it covered. But short of blowing his lair up around him, they were forced to lay siege and wait. No action would be taken until new orders were issued, at least twelve hours from now.

He tapped a few keys to signal that the message was received.

Alexia wasn't going to like the news.

Nor, he remembered, was he supposed to tell her.

The message was in code, so she wouldn't have to know. Wouldn't have to worry. His brain raced, pulling together a plan. He'd make her some hot chocolate, dim the lights and talk her into going to sleep.

It wasn't a very elaborate plan, but sometimes simple was best.

"What's going on?" she asked.

"Just a weather report," he said, tapping the screen. "It looks like it's going to snow."

"Ha-ha." Giving him a narrow look, she got stiffly to her feet and, after taking a second to bend in half and touch her toes, she crossed to the bank of radios and monitors and peered at the message.

"A weather report? Seriously?"

"SOP is to check in every two hours. A weather report is a simple message to use. If it was somehow intercepted, it says nothing. And it's always good to know the weather."

He couldn't tell if she was buying it or not. That was the trouble with Alexia. Half the time, she was an open book, easy to read and ready to share. The other half made him feel like an untrained schoolboy trying to talk to his first girl. Clueless and inept.

"Well, at least the navy has a handle on the weather," she finally said.

His shoulders relaxed and he let out the breath he hadn't realized he was holding. He didn't want her worrying. Which would be fine if it was because her worrying would make the mission more difficult. But he knew that wasn't why. It was because he hated the idea of her suffering in any way.

Cade was right. He had a problem.

"Ready for some hot chocolate?" he asked, doing what

he always did when faced with a problem. Taking it down one step at a time.

"Sure." She glanced at the now-blank screen again, then followed him over to take her seat at the table. "Can I help? It seems like you're always cooking for me."

That's because with the exception of the field rations they'd just had, he'd ended up eating a bit of every meal off her naked body.

Don't go there, he warned himself. His imagination didn't listen, though. As he heated the water to mix with powdered milk, his brain threw out a dozen or so images of the way Alexia had looked covered in plum jelly. Or in cream sauce. Or in soapy bubbles that slid, slow and thick, down her bare breast. The tip beaded in pouting delight, just waiting for his tongue.

"Shit," he muttered, shaking the splash of hot water off his hand. *Focus, dammit.* He removed the pot of boiling water from the burner, dumped the white powder in and stirred.

"You're making a mess," Alexia said, tilted almost sideways in her chair so she could see what he was doing. "Are you sure I can't help?"

Blake looked down at the table. The burner was sizzling with specks of watery milk. Powder pooled around the pot like mounds of snow. He'd stirred so hard that the back of his hand looked as if he had white freckles.

"Here," he said, pushing the pot, spoon and chocolate powder toward her. "Have at it."

Needing to move, wishing for action—any action that didn't involve Alexia's naked body—he strode over to the monitors to check the display, then to the tent flap, pulling down the pseudocurtain and looking out.

It was still white.

Go figure.

"Did you want some?"

Some of her? Oh, yeah.

"No. Thanks," he added, trying to soften the bark. He glanced back to see she'd poured half the mixture into a tin cup. She held up the pot, looking at him questioningly.

He really needed to get a grip. This was just an adrenaline-induced loss of control, combined with seeing someone he'd been obsessing over. No big deal.

Time for phase two of his plan. Get her the hell to sleep.

He crossed the tent, reaching for the pot. Their fingers brushed. He wanted more. He was desperate to touch her again. Even if it was only her fingertips or her hair. He still had dreams about that hair. She'd brushed it back into some twisting rope, the red glowing in the soft lamplight. He remembered the feel of her hair in his hands, trailing down his body. The silky feel, the sweet scent.

In an instant, he went from soldier to man.

Horny, turned on and ready to rock, man.

"How is it?" he asked, his voice a little hoarse.

"Surprisingly good." She sipped again, then arched one brow. "Are you sure you won't have some?"

"I'm still full from dinner," he said. And desperate for more space than the small tent allowed. "But you must be exhausted. Why don't you finish your drink, then try to get some rest."

"I was hoping we could chat." Her smile was sweetly mischievous, making Blake want to howl and beat on something. She was supposed to be overwrought. Not cute, dammit. He'd never had to fight off all these sexual and emotional needs while he was on duty before. And couldn't say he was liking the new experience much.

"Chat? About what?" he asked.

"I thought we'd talk about why you were assigned

this mission. If hand-holding isn't your usual thing, then what is?"

"I'm the radioman. Communications, languages, they're my usual things."

"That's kind of funny," she said in a tone that didn't sound as if she was enjoying the humor. She stared into her cup for a second, then met his eyes. "We're both communications specialists."

She stopped there, as if she were standing against the door between now and then and wasn't sure she wanted to open it.

"And you think we didn't communicate," he said, figuring they had to step through the door sooner or later.

"You think we did?" she asked.

Her tone wasn't challenging. It was simply curious. He wondered if she'd burned through her supply of negative emotions. He'd seen it before. It was like watching someone hit rock bottom, so they operated in an emotional vacuum. It wouldn't last. But as chickenshit as it was, he sure hoped they were picked up before she tapped into a new supply.

He hesitated before responding, though. There was a good chance she still had plenty of mad tucked away in there. And despite his wanting distance between them, this was a damn small tent to be sharing with a pissed-off woman. Still, he could only answer honestly.

"I thought we communicated just fine. We were focused on one thing, and we got our wants and needs across to each other pretty damn well."

Something flared in her dark eyes. Interest. Heat. A dangerous curiosity. Blake braced himself. But as quick as it'd flamed, she banked it. With short, deliberate moves, she set the cup on the table and got to her feet.

"It just hit me how exhausted I am. I'm going to go ahead and sleep."

He didn't let the relief pour in until she'd climbed onto the cot, still fully clothed, and covered herself with the thermal blanket. To help her along, he dimmed all the lights.

"Good night," he said quietly.

She didn't answer for a second. Then, her voice a sigh, she said, "'Night. And thank you."

11

BLAKE LISTENED to Alexia's breathing. As if he could coax her into relaxing, he breathed along with her, slowing, soothing. After a few minutes, he knew she was asleep.

That's when he let himself relax.

He should sleep. The perimeter alarms were on. If anything heavier than snow crossed them, he'd know. Still, he hesitated. He didn't trust Alexia's safety to machines.

For just a second, he let his frustration at being on this side, tucked away from the action, pound through him. He wasn't made for sitting it out. Not even with a beautiful woman.

His watch set to ping him in thirty minutes, he forced himself to sink into the cot. Eyes closed, he tried to put everything—especially the woman sleeping three feet away—out of his mind. If he wanted to keep her safe, he had to be in top form. To be in top form, he needed sleep. He wouldn't sleep if he was imagining her naked except for those leather combat boots.

It was the boots that did it. He focused all his attention on those, and slowly felt himself sinking into a doze. He was a breath away from sleep when he heard something.

He jackknifed up and flew from his cot. He pulled a sobbing Alexia into his arms.

"Baby, it's okay," he soothed, brushing the damp tendrils of hair off her face. By the lights of the monitors, he could see the terror in her eyes. "There's nothing to worry about anymore. I'm here. I've got you."

"Hold me," she begged, wrapping her arms so tightly around his waist, his breath shortened. "Don't let me go. Don't let anything happen."

"I'm holding you." To back up his claim, he ran his hands up and down the back of her thick sweater.

"Hold me tighter. I've never been so scared, Blake. I close my eyes and I can see him again. See the glee in his nasty rat face as he threatened me. He promised to let his men do horrible things to me."

Fury pounded through him, racing past frustration and damn near knocking out his control.

"You're safe," he told her again, brushing a kiss against the silkiness of her hair.

He didn't know if it was because she needed the assurance of seeing his expression, or if it was a reaction to that kiss. But Alexia peeled her cheek off his chest and leaned back. Just far enough that they could look into each other's eyes. Feel each other's breath on their faces. Blake knew he should get up. He was on duty. He was sworn to protect her. Hell, her father had handpicked him to keep her safe.

Every reason—and there were a lot—that he should get the hell up and away from her crossed his mind.

He looked into her eyes, the dark heat there calling to him, touching something in his heart that he couldn't resist.

"Just letting you know ahead of time, this is a huge mistake and I'm sorry," he said.

Her brow furrowed, but before she could ask what he meant, he kissed her.

IT WAS LIKE WAKING from a nightmare and finding herself safe, cocooned in pleasure. Like coming home. As Blake's lips sank into hers, Alexia felt right for the first time in months. His mouth was so soft, so sweet. His body so warm and hard as his arms enfolded her and held her close.

She wanted more. Needed him with a desperate, clawing need. With him, she was safe. With him, she was whole.

Her mouth moved under his, their lips sliding together then slipping apart. At his touch, the tension and terror that had gripped her fell away. At his kiss, the horrified images of the last four days dissipated, like smoke.

He was heaven, pure and simple. It was as if nothing could scare her, nothing could hurt her as long as he was close.

Slowly, he released her lips and pulled away. Her fingers clutched his shoulders, trying to keep him from moving, from leaving.

"You were crying," he said, his fingers gently wiping dampness she hadn't even realized was streaked over her cheeks before sliding along her hair to cup the back of her head.

Well, that was hot. Nothing sexier than sobbing in your sleep. Alexia frowned, her shoulders drooping, right along with her sexual bubble.

"That's why you kissed me? Because I was crying?"

He hesitated. She could tell he was debating. The easy way, or the truth. She should make it simpler for him. After all, the man had rescued her from a stinking lunatic. But she wanted more, she wanted…well, hard. Him hard. Better yet, him hard inside her.

"I kissed you because I couldn't resist," he said, his fingers now sliding into the braid at the back of her head, loosening her hair, massaging her scalp in a way that made her want to purr. "I shouldn't have, though."

The tension that had been building again started to fade. Joy bubbled up, filling her smile with a little extra sparkle. Excitement started growing again as the hope of sex, and yes, those incredible fingers, worked their magic.

"Why not?" she whispered, her hands roaming his back, delighting in the play of strong muscles beneath his shirt. Her reasons why not were a mile long.

Better to focus on his reasons instead. That way she could brush them aside and get on to the good stuff.

"Because you're you and I'm me."

"Ah." Alexia couldn't help it. She laughed. "That's succinct."

His lips twitched, but he didn't smile. He gave her a serious, peering-all-the-way-into-her-soul kind of look instead.

"You're the admiral's daughter. I'm a SEAL. You're looking for a transparent, open relationship. I live in the shadows. You're the victim under my protection. I'm charged with the mission of getting you home safe."

As if his words had flipped open the tent flap, the chill of reality crept over her. Alexia's fingers stopped caressing his back, then slowly fell away.

Looked as if their lists were pretty similar after all.

"Well, those are some solid reasons," she acknowledged quietly. How could she argue with her own justifications? If they both had them, they were even more rational than just her making them up in her own head, right?

Alexia sighed, wishing she could go back to believing that she was overreacting.

On his face she saw the same frustration, the same reluctance that she felt. He eased away.

She shivered, her body instantly missing his warmth. She wanted to pull the blankets around her, but doing so would mean he had to move. And sex or no sex, she wanted—needed—him close for as long as she could keep him.

"Yeah. Good solid reasons why we should keep things smart," he said, sitting upright. He shoved one hand through his hair, making it stand up in short spikes, and gave Alexia a stiff smile. The only reason she was able to smile back was because she could see that stiffness echoed in his tented fatigues.

Her breath caught in her chest, adding to the surreal buzzing she heard in her head. It was like standing, starving, outside a bakery, staring at a window display of her very favorite, most decadently delicious pastries. Or in this case, cannoli. Her eyes traced the ridge of his pants and she corrected that to jumbo cannoli.

"Smart is good," she agreed absently.

"Smart is necessary," he told her, his words a little more clipped than usual. He was only saying them because it was *the right thing to do,* she realized.

"We're two intelligent, mature adults who know how to control our urges." Her fingers traced a design on his thigh, reveling in the corded muscles she could feel, even through the heavy cotton of his pants. Slowly, as if she was sneaking up on it, her fingers trailed closer and closer to the ridge of his impressive erection.

His gaze narrowed, eyes calculating. As if he was figuring out just how to turn this to their advantage. Their *naked* advantage.

"Just because there's this thing with us," he said, waving his fingers back and forth between them as if there were an electric field there, "that doesn't mean we have to give in to it."

"Of course not," she agreed with a strained laugh, her nipples aching and heavy as every breath brushed them against the thermal fabric of her shirt. "We're not animals, after all."

"Nope. Not animals," he agreed, his eyes locking on her sweater-covered breasts, heating. Making her nipples tighten even more. "We know better than to get into something that we've both clearly accepted is bad for us."

"So bad," she breathed, her eyes lifting from his crotch to meet his slumberous gaze. "So, so bad."

"So we're having wild, uncontrolled animal sex, right?" he asked, his hand reaching out to hover over—but not quite touch, dammit—her aching nipple.

"Oh, yeah. Hurry and get your pants off," she ordered, saving time by yanking two sweaters at once over her head. When her face cleared the fabric, she saw that Blake had pulled off his long-sleeved T-shirt and was unlacing his boots. What was with military footwear? she wondered, wanting to cuss at how long it took. Clearly, whoever designed it didn't have fast sex in mind.

For the first time since they'd met, Blake showed a lack of grace as he hopped on one foot, trying to untangle the mile-long laces on his snow boots.

Wanting to hurry him along, Alexia took a deep breath and yanked her thermal undershirt over her head. Braless, since she'd thrown out everything she'd been wearing in that hellhole, her torso was instantly covered in goose bumps.

Until Blake's gaze, hot and intense, warmed her like a caress.

"Damn, you're gorgeous," he breathed.

Then he lost his balance and toppled onto the other cot.

The crash was deafening.

She paused, her pants unzipped and her hands on her hips to shove them down, and met his eyes.

Desperation turned to laughter. Her gaze still locked on

his, Alexia clapped her hand to her mouth to try to contain the chortles. But when he grinned, she couldn't hold back.

Giggling, she pulled the blanket over her nudity and shifted into a sitting position to peer at Blake. Already on his feet—gotta love that physical conditioning—he was pulling the cot back into an upright position.

"Are you okay?" she asked as soon as she got control of herself.

"Yeah, but the cot's a little worse for wear." He kicked at one of the legs with his stocking-clad foot to indicate the bent metal.

"Oops." Alexia wrinkled her nose at the damage.

"Can't say I don't know how to show you romance," he told her, still smiling.

"Well, one of us was definitely swept off their feet." Then she hesitated. Without the haze of his sweet rescue of her from her nightmare, or the reckless desperation that had pushed them toward fast-and-furious sex, they were left with… What?

A choice.

Alexia's gaze fell to the plain black wool blanket she'd wrapped herself in, her fingers twisting then untwisting the hem.

She felt, rather than saw, Blake drop to his haunches next to her cot. Slowly, after taking a fortifying breath, she lifted her gaze to his.

He was so damn gorgeous. Blue eyes so warm, so inviting, and a mouth that was sexy whether he was smiling or frowning. Sexiest on hers, though. She could see the patience in his gaze. The comfortable acceptance that this was her choice.

It'd been so hard to get over him last time. She'd shoved her feelings about him, her wishes and regrets and longings, all into a box in the back corner of her mind. Then she'd pretended it didn't exist. All but the anger. That, she'd held on to. Used as a weapon to beat down any thoughts she had of maybe peeking into that box.

This time, though, she wouldn't have that anger. This time, she couldn't blame him for anything that wasn't his fault, as she had before.

This time, she was accepting him exactly as he was, completely aware of his loyalties. If they had sex, *this time* she was one hundred percent responsible for her choice. For her feelings. For whatever happened next.

Alexia's fingers shook a little as she stared into his eyes. There, she saw acceptance, appreciation and a heat that went deeper than passion. A heat she couldn't resist. Terrified, but unable to do otherwise, she dropped the blanket and opened her arms.

Blake gave an appreciative moan, traced his finger around one areola, then the other. Looking as if he was about to partake in the Fountain of Youth, he leaned forward to sip delicately.

Alexia's own moan was high and breathless.

Then he moved. Rising to his feet, he stood like a warrior god of old, his broad shoulders tapering in a golden line down to his slender waist. His cock jutted proudly over thick, muscled thighs. Unable to resist, Alexia lifted herself to one elbow and leaned forward to blow lightly on the straining tip of his erection.

It jumped, as if coming to attention.

She slanted him a wicked look, then leaned closer to run her tongue around the velvety head. His fists clenched at his hips, but he didn't move. Didn't try to take control.

"Yum," she murmured before taking him into her mouth, sliding her lips on and down the hard length of him. His fingers splayed, as if he was going to grab her, then he fisted them again. As a reward, she sucked, hard, just the tip, and made him groan out loud.

"My turn," he insisted, lowering himself to the cot and sliding over her body. "Otherwise you might not get yours."

"Oh, I'll get mine," she guaranteed, her bare feet skimming up the back of his hard thighs before she dug her heels into his butt and pressed her aching core to his erection. "You're going to give it to me."

"Yeah. I'm going to give it to you all right." His teasing smile was the last thing she saw before his mouth covered hers. All it took was the touch of his tongue against hers and Alexia went crazy. She needed him. All of him.

"Now," she demanded.

"I'm not done," he said with a strained laugh as his fingers slipped between their bodies and down her belly to cup her curls.

As soon as he touched her swollen clitoris, she shattered. Stars burst, heat exploded. Her entire body convulsed, trembling with the power of her orgasm.

He moved like lightning, thrusting into her with a low, animalistic growl that turned her on even more. He took her hands in his, dragging both their arms over her head. Their eyes locked as his body rose over hers. Excitement swirled, deep and low in Alexia's belly. Every nerve ending was electrified, raw with pleasure. Blake arched his back, then slid into her again in one deliciously slow thrust.

Her body contracted around him, reveling in the feel of his hard length as it moved in, out, in. Slow. So slow she could count her heartbeats between thrusts. So slow she wanted to cry from the pleasure of it.

He pulled her hands higher. Alexia gasped, arching her back against the pressure. She shifted onto her heels. The angle change meant the length of his cock now slid against her G-spot, that electrified, pleasure-charged sensor sending tight, tingling spirals of pleasure up, higher and higher in her belly. Blake bent his head, taking the beaded, aching tip of her breast into his mouth. The spirals climbed higher, grasped tighter.

Her breath came in pants now. Passion swirled, gripping her. Her body tensed as he teased her nipple deep into his mouth, then sucked. When the edge of his teeth scraped along the sensitive flesh, she exploded.

She wanted to close her eyes. To escape into the decadent ecstasy as it washed over her, pulling her deeper and deeper into delight.

But Blake wouldn't release her gaze. Like a magnet, he held tight, forcing her to let him watch her orgasm, to see all the way into her soul as she let go.

As she exploded. Her body, her emotions, the very core of her being all laid bare to him as passion took over. She whimpered at the power, unable to do anything but feel. And it felt incredible.

Slowly, drifting like a downy feather, she floated back to earth. Her heartbeat was still so loud in her head she couldn't hear a thing. But awareness was returning to her body. A body that was still shivering with the aftershocks of pleasure, like mini-orgasms rippling through her.

And no wonder.

Blake was still inside her. Still moving, slow and steady. Building, tantalizing. Teasing her with his control.

Time to shift the balance of power, she decided.

She reached up, threading her fingers through his short hair, and pulled his mouth to hers. Her kiss was sweet at first. A gentle thank-you for the delectable orgasm.

Then, as he sank into it, she took it deeper. Her tongue stabbed, her teeth nipped. He stiffened, the smooth rhythm of his thrusts shifting. Jerking.

Alexia let go of his hair, pushing against his shoulders.

Then, in a move that made her grateful for her thrice-weekly pilates class, she gave a big push, and switched positions so she was on top.

"Yum," she whispered.

A wicked smile played about his kiss-swollen lips and he gave an appreciative nod. "Yum, indeed."

He angled his body so he was half raised, his head leaning against the wall of the tent, his hands cupping both her breasts. Holding them in position for his mouth.

Alexia wrapped her legs around the back of his hips, her heels digging into his butt.

Then she set the pace.

Fast. Intense. His face tightened as he drove into her.

"Now," he demanded in a low, guttural tone. His face drawn taut, his muscles tense, he stared into her eyes.

She'd never felt such intimacy, such a touching of souls, as she did in that second. Blake, the connection between them, had become her entire world. Her entire focus.

He thrust harder. His eyes narrowed. He sucked air through his teeth. Feeling more powerful than ever before in her life, Alexia shifted higher, swirling her hips to meet his. Then she clenched her core muscles, grabbing his cock, holding tight.

He exploded.

Hers, she thought as his breath caught.

He was all hers. And she didn't want to let him go.

Ever.

BLAKE WAS ENGULFED by the intensity of the passion pounding through his veins. The orgasm grabbed ahold, ambushing him with its power. As he poured himself into Alexia's warmth, his body shuddered, his arms shaking as his muscles tensed to the point of shattering.

His orgasm triggered hers. Still spinning out of control,

he watched through narrow, passion-blurred eyes as she went over. Her body tensed, arching her back. Her breasts, lush and gorgeous, bobbed in time with her frenzied gyrations. She tilted her head back, her moans filling the tent. Filling him with power, his ego swelling so he felt like a he-man. All-powerful, totally awesome.

"Wow," she breathed a few seconds later, staring down at him. Damp tendrils of hair stuck to her face, her skin glistening in the dim light. Slowly, as if all her bones had melted, she sank onto his chest.

"Definitely wow," he agreed, lifting her chin for a kiss. He wanted to say more. To find words to express how incredible he felt with her, how great that had been. But he couldn't. Besides, she looked exhausted.

Telling himself it was the gentlemanly thing to do and not chickenshit, he kissed her again, then rolled so they were on their sides.

She curled into his body as if they were one. Blake closed his eyes against the emotions buffeting him. Passion, still flaming hot, led the pack. But right behind it was a tenderness, a gentle sort of sweetness he'd never felt before. It scared the hell out of him, so he focused on the passion instead.

He wrapped his arms tight around her, giving himself a brief moment of sweet surrender before he hitched her higher, his lips latching on to her breast.

"What are you doing?" she gasped, sounding half asleep.

"I'm not finished."

"Oh, yes, you are," she said with a gasping sort of laugh, her fingers digging into his shoulders. "I felt you finish, bud. Don't try to claim otherwise."

Kissing her, a soft, gentle brush of his lips over the swell of her breast, he gave her a wicked look. "I would never claim that was anything but fabulous. But I'm not finished."

"You've got to be kidding."

Then his fingers found her. Still wet and swollen, he flicked his thumb over her quivering clitoris. She gasped, her head falling back against the pillow and her nails leaving tiny crescents in his skin.

"You're not kidding," she breathed. "How..."

Her words trailed off when he slid lower, kissing his way down the center of her body. When he reached the flaming curls at her apex, she moaned, shaking her head as if she couldn't believe he was there. But her thighs fell to the side, making room for his shoulders.

This time, when he emptied himself in her, he knew he was done. There. He'd given her all he had.

Every drop.

Every bit of pleasure.

Every ounce of himself.

He collapsed, pulling her tighter into his arms and rolling so he wouldn't crush her. It was all he could do not to groan out loud as he realized what he'd done.

He'd gone and fallen in love.

He was so screwed.

_12_

BLAKE CURLED HIS BODY behind Alexia's, his arms wrapped around her waist and fingers twined with hers. It was the closest he could get without being inside her. But give him another five, maybe ten minutes, and he'd be up for that again, too.

She was quiet in his arms. Too quiet. He could tell she wasn't floating on a cloud in sexual nirvana. Not with all the tension he could feel radiating off her.

Give him another five, maybe ten minutes, and he'd get rid of that, too.

"You never asked me what happened at the compound," she finally said, her words painfully low. "Is that a part of your orders? You're on pickup-and-delivery service, but not allowed to know what's in the package?"

Protocol clearly stated that he was exactly what she'd said—pickup and delivery. His orders had been clear. Don't grill her. Debriefing would be done by higher-ups. Besides, Blake winced, trauma, PTS—she was going to be carting around plenty. But he wasn't equipped to deal with it. Hell, with her psych degree, she was better prepared than he was.

Distract and delay, he decided. Until she could talk to someone who knew how to guide her back to feeling safe.

"I'm pretty sure I just explored the package pretty thoroughly," Blake said, laughing a little before he leaned down to gently bite the back of her shoulder. Ah, the perfect distraction. Alexia gave a delighted shudder, pressing her hips back against him. He felt life stirring again, and was tempted. Oh, so tempted to let their bodies take over again.

But even though they didn't have a future, even though his reasons for them not being together were all still strong and solid, he couldn't do it. He couldn't go the same route he had before. He'd seen the questions in her eyes last fall, had known she wanted to talk, to connect in more than just a physical way. He could use the typical guy excuse that talking about emotions was stupid, a total girlie thing. But he knew that wasn't what she was looking for. She just wanted to know more about the guy she was sleeping with than his favorite position and what moves sent him over the edge.

Blake had hurt Alexia once because he'd taken the easy route. He wasn't going to do it again if he could help it.

"SOP in a rescue is to get in, get the victim and get out. We're not supposed to ask questions unless it pertains to completing the mission," he explained.

"Is that what I am? A *standard operating procedure?*" She didn't sound angry. Nor did her body stiffen or shift away. She simply looked at him with patient curiosity. As if she could wait, that she totally trusted he'd get to the right answer eventually.

Blake frowned. Why didn't she ever react the way he expected? They had sex, and instead of falling into a satisfied stupor, she started thinking about her captivity. He inadvertently labeled her and she laughed it off. Would he ever understand how her mind worked? What her emotional triggers were?

"There's nothing standard about you," he said honestly. "The truth is, I don't do this kind of thing well."

She twisted in his arms so they were face-to-face. Her hair, free of the braid again, haloed around them like red flames. Her slender shoulders and silky skin made for a gorgeous distraction. Blake wanted to pull her tight against him, to tuck her head into his chest and distract her with sex. But the way she was staring at him made it clear she wasn't going to go for it.

"What kind of thing?"

"The emotional aftermath," he said with an uncomfortable shrug. "Dealing with the trauma. You went through hell. You deserve to talk to someone who understands how to guide you through the healing process. I'd say the wrong thing, or pat your head because I don't know how to react, or cuss and punch something. And you don't need anyone making it worse for you."

Her eyes turned to liquid, her smile trembling a little at the corners.

"You are so sweet," she said quietly, brushing her fingertips over his lips in a whisper-soft touch almost as intimate as a kiss.

"No. I just don't want to talk the emotional stuff," he dismissed gruffly. But inside, he felt like a little boy doing backflips. All excited because she thought he was sweet.

"But you would, wouldn't you? If I had to talk it through, if I couldn't wait for a professional who knew how to counsel me, you'd let me work it through with you?"

Blake would rather take a bullet. But, keeping his cringe inside, he nodded.

Her smile was bright enough to light the entire tent. With a husky laugh, she hugged him tight. Her bare breasts pressed temptingly against his chest while her legs twined with his.

"Sweet," she told him. "You are so seriously sweet. Sweet enough that I won't put you through that."

"Thank you," Blake breathed. Then, because words weren't enough, he leaned down to kiss her. Their lips melted together, heating him through and through.

Maybe their five-minute wait was up...

Before he could find out, she leaned back to break the kiss and smiled again.

"So all that hand-holding you do is restricted to the rescue," she teased. "Not the recovery?"

"We should all do what we do best. And leave the things we do worst for someone else."

"And what do you do best?"

"Whatever I set my mind to," he told her. It wasn't bragging. He was damn good at what he did.

"Do you ever worry?" she asked, her fingers tracing a pattern on his chest, but her eyes locked on his. "Does it ever just seem like it's too much? The constant living on edge, the missions and danger and never knowing what's next?"

"It's my life. Danger, the unexpected. They're second nature. Like breathing." Unable to resist those lips, already swollen from his kisses, Blake leaned down to kiss her again.

When he leaned back, she gave him a look that said no distractions allowed. Blake was tempted to see how long it would take to make that look change into passionate surrender.

But finally, with those patient eyes locked on his, he sighed and admitted, "Yeah, sometimes. I didn't used to worry. I'm serious when I say it's a job. I'm highly trained, and damn good at what I do. So doing it isn't a worry."

"But?"

How did she know there was a but? He replayed his words, his tone. There hadn't been a but in there, dammit.

"You know, you wasted that psych degree of yours," he teased, trying to laugh it off.

Despite her smile, she suddenly looked sad. Stressed. He could feel the tension tightening in her lower back.

"What?" he asked. "Why does that bother you?"

"That's what my father said the last time he spoke to me. He wanted me planted somewhere safe and sound, billing fifty-minute hours and poking into people's heads."

Weird. Blake hadn't taken the admiral to be a touchy-feely, get-in-touch-with-yourself kind of guy.

"I guess parents have their own vision for our lives, and it doesn't always mesh with our own."

"Or we have a vision for our own life that doesn't fit theirs," she said, her words only a little bitter.

Same thing, he started to say. Then he realized it wasn't.

"Did yours?" she asked, her fingers tracing a design on his chest. Sliding lower, tighter.

"Did mine what?" he responded absently, all his attention focused on where she'd touch next.

"Did your parents' vision suit you? Or did your vision suit them?"

Her fingers forgotten, Blake snorted. "I didn't rate high enough to merit visions. My old man walked out when I was three, and my mother's view was usually blurred by vodka. She didn't care what I did. Or what I didn't do."

Alexia's fingers shifted upward, teasing the hair on his chest, then rubbing in sweet, soothing circles.

"She must be proud now, though, right? You've been decorated so many times. Won so many honors."

Blake arched a brow. How did she know what he'd done?

She looked stubborn for a second, then sniffed. "So I checked your records. So what?"

He couldn't help it. He laughed, then kissed the tip of her nose. She was so freaking cute. Her sexiness was blatant, always right there like a punch in the face. Her brains were subtle, a backdrop to the sexy. Again, always there, but not something she shoved down your throat. But the cuteness? The vulnerable sweetness? That's what got to him. She hid it a lot of the time, so when it peeked out, it was extra special.

"So I'm glad you were curious enough to want to check me out," he said softly. Then he grimaced. He didn't want to talk about his past. It wasn't something he was ashamed of, but it wasn't his world anymore. Still, honesty deserved honesty, so he told her, "My mother doesn't care about any of that. I'm not even sure she knows I made the SEAL team. When I refused to send home my paycheck, she wrote me off. Said we were through. It's been six years and I can't say I miss her."

Horror, anger and a sort of recognition all mixed together in Alexia's expression. She kissed his chin, as if kissing away any hurt he might still feel.

"Even when we don't care, it still hurts when they close that door, doesn't it?" she said quietly.

Blake frowned.

"What doors are closed to you?" he asked, even though he was pretty sure he knew. He hated that the admiral, a man he honestly looked up to and thought a great deal of, could be so flawed as a father.

"My father disowned me last fall. Again."

Last fall?

Shit.

"Because of me?"

Her smile was pure appreciation.

"No, although my unacceptable behavior toward you did trigger the discussion."

"By discussion you mean fight?"

Alexia gave him a sardonic look. "I thought you knew my father. One doesn't fight with the admiral. One listens. One obeys. Or one is disowned."

"I was the trigger. What was the bullet?"

"He doesn't find my career acceptable. It's embarrassing to him and my mother that I focus on sexual behavior. They'd rather I use my psych degree working for the government. Or barring that, they want me to go into private practice in a tidy little office somewhere and talk sexual behavior behind closed doors, where it belongs."

"But you said what you're doing will help a lot of people."

"It will. In the last year, it has, actually. We just received a huge grant to further the work, which is probably what brought the wrong kind of attention." She was quiet for a second, then shifted one shoulder as if it didn't matter. "Fitting, my father would say. To my parents, subliminal programming to heal sexual aberrations is nothing more than *self-indulgence for the weak*."

"That's bullshit." It pissed him off that she would blame herself, even in a roundabout way, for the kidnapping, or for her parents' narrow views. "You make a difference. And you love what you do. Don't let bullies push you into sidestepping that passion. Even if one of them is a terrorist and the other your father."

Alexia's tension faded, her body relaxing into his again as she laughed.

"I guess that's what you do, isn't it? Stop tyrants from getting away with bullying."

"That's one of our specialties," he confirmed. Blake was always proud to be a SEAL, to serve his country. But seeing the admiration in Alexia's eyes added a nice layer of muscle to that pride.

"So why did things change?" Her tone was pure compassion, so understanding and sweet that he wanted to lay his head on her shoulder and let every pain he'd ever had drain away. "You said you don't worry about doing your job. But you worry about something else now, don't you?"

Blake went as still as if she'd pulled the pin from a grenade and tossed it to him. One wrong move and there would be emotional spattering, all over the place.

"Maybe you can sideline with that psych degree," he joked stiffly, wondering how the hell she'd circled back. Hadn't baring her own woes been a distraction? You'd think the sad, pathetic story of his childhood was enough to listen to. She still wanted more?

"You don't have to tell me," she said, sounding compassionate and soothing. He could feel the hurt in the set of her shoulders, though. See it in the stiffness of her smile. "I just, well, you were hurting before. Last fall. It made me sad to see the unhappiness in your eyes."

Blake clenched his jaw. She'd known then that he was hurting? Was he that transparent? For just a second, he frowned. That wasn't why she'd slept with him, was it? Pity sex? As quick as the thought came in, it faded. There had been nothing pitiful between them, and he'd be a fool to start thinking that way.

"That was a rough time," he said, figuring he could let it go at that. Then, hoping she'd accept it as enough of an excuse, he added, "I'd served on three back-to-back missions and was hitting burnout."

"That's got to be hard. Like an adrenaline rush that doesn't stop. I'd think you'd face quite a lot of exhaustion." She sounded so understanding that Blake had to close his eyes against the emotions her compassion unleashed. He wanted to kick himself. He'd had access to this much caring, this much sympathy eight months ago. And instead of opening to her, he'd locked everything up tight, deep inside where it could fester and ferment and grow. Damn, he was smart.

"You don't really notice the exhaustion," he heard himself saying. "At first, the back-to-back element gives you an edge. You're always on, always primed. That makes for a pretty effective weapon."

"But after a while, a bow drawn taut loses its intensity, doesn't it?"

He nodded. "Yeah. That's when things happen."

"What happened?" she whispered, her words a breath of comfort over him. No demand, no surprise, it was as if she'd known there was something aching there and she wasn't going to pry it loose, but simply wait until it surfaced so she could scoop it away.

"We lost a guy."

He watched her face as he said it. Waited for the judgment. The shock or horror. But her expression didn't change. Her dark eyes might have melted a little more, but that was all. Instead, she shifted, leaning closer to brush a soft kiss over his lips.

Comfort.

Healing.

Acceptance.

For the first time since he'd watched the life drain out of his buddy, Blake felt those things. All because of a tiny little kiss.

No, he realized.

Because of Alexia.

He waited. Now that the door was open, she'd ask questions. She was intuitive enough to sense his loss was more than just a team member—although that'd be devastating enough. She'd make him talk about Phil. About what he'd meant, how hard it was to adjust to life without him.

Blake's stomach, cast iron in battle, shuddered.

"That has to haunt you," she said quietly. "And make you second-guess your decisions, be extra cautious when it's costing you to slow down and be careful."

Blake drew back to stare at her. That wasn't prodding and poking. That wasn't pushing him into facing things. Where was the emotional aggression? She was trying to kill him, wasn't she? Or worse, make him fall in love with her.

"You need to remember that life's short," she said, her palm skimming his cheek. "We don't get to pick the how or the where. All we get to do is live the days we're given to the fullest."

Blake had fallen off a cliff once. You'd think it would be a wild and fast plummet to the ground, filled with fear of the pain that was surely waiting on impact. And it had been. But it had also been surreal, a time to assess every decision, every mistake and totally analyze the misstep that had brought him into the free fall. It was oddly comforting to know that dive to the death provided plenty of time for regret.

That's how he felt right now. He was falling. He could feel it and knew there was no reversing the direction, no halting the fast plunge. That the landing was going to hurt was unquestionable. That he'd regret not watching his step was guaranteed.

Yet, for all that, if someone tossed him a rope to haul him back to safety, he'd have refused. Because some things just had to happen.

Like falling in love with Alexia.

BLAKE WAS LOOKING at her as if he could see all the way into her soul. As if he knew what was in her heart and was waiting for a confession. Alexia swallowed, wondering what had just happened. And how she was going to deal with it. Because whatever it was, it felt huge.

And she didn't mean the erection rubbing against her thigh.

She figured she had three options.

Reach down and slide her fingers over that erection, so they both changed focus to something a lot more pleasurable.

Voice any of the dozens of questions clamoring in her mind, like, who had died? How close had Blake been to him? How was he dealing with the loss after all these months? And oh so many more nosy, prying queries.

Or she could face her own fears and ask him what he was feeling. Ask him what it was like to face the death of someone he cared about, and how he could keep on when he could be next.

She could ask him if she was just an escape, a way to get his mind off those worries. A warm pair of arms and an easy distraction. Or if she was more. If they could be more, together.

That last one was a little terrifying.

Could she deal with whatever he was feeling? Was she ready to hear it? If she asked Blake to open that door, she'd have no choice but to face whatever emotions were on the other side. And then, in the name of fairness, she'd have to give him access to her emotional closet, too. That secret place where she stashed all the feelings she was too afraid to deal with.

She wanted to go with the first option. But she knew she'd hate herself if she didn't at least try to open the emotional door.

"Since life is so short," she said, picking up from the

last comment she'd made, "don't you think it's important to be honest about what you want?"

"I honestly want you," he said, his words teasing, but the look in his eyes deep and intense.

And there she was, back to choosing between the easy route—sex—or the harder one of emotional honesty. Before Blake, Alexia would have sworn that she'd always pick emotional honesty. But it was easy to think that when there was very little at stake.

She took a deep breath, then asked, "And what else, besides me, do you want?"

She figured he'd sidestep. Dance away or turn the query back to something sexy. A part of her hoped he would. Then she'd know she'd tried, given it her best, but that it was all his fault they couldn't dive into the messy, core-wrenching pain of honest feelings.

"I want to make a difference. I want to know I've done my best." He looked past her for a second, as if he was scanning his want list. Then he met her eyes again, and made Alexia's heart stutter. "I want a full life. One that's more than just the military. I want a home. Someplace, someone that accepts me for who I am. For what I am."

Stuttering just a second ago, now her heart tripped, not sure if it should run toward him or skitter away in fear. He wanted everything. And she knew he'd give everything in return.

Frozen, more afraid in that second than she'd been when the rat terrorist had offered her up to his henchman, Alexia tried to figure out what to say.

Suddenly a loud buzz rang out. Lights flashed.

Blake's expression shifted from sexy man to soldier in the blink of an eye as he looked past her shoulder toward the equipment bank.

Fear, already hunkered down in her belly, exploded.

"Is that them? Did they find us?"

"No," he assured her, sliding from her arms and the cot. He moved toward the equipment, grabbing his pants as he went. "It's just a message. We check in every couple of hours, remember. Nothing to worry about."

Bless the navy, she thought as the tension poured out of her, leaving her limp and exhausted. Maybe after some sleep in her own bed, some time to sort through her own thoughts, she'd be ready to talk emotions with him. Ready to share what she felt—hell, maybe she'd know what she felt.

But right now, this second? She was just grateful for the interruption.

She watched him answer the radio call, too relieved at the emotional escape that she wasn't even curious about the message.

Then she shivered. Without his body there keeping her warm, she was chillingly aware that she was naked. She tugged the blanket closer, but it didn't help. As she watched him pull his shirt over his head and tuck it into his fatigues, she reluctantly reached for her own clothes.

Interruption or not, they were going to have to finish that conversation. It would have been so much easier naked.

She'd got as far as tugging the second pair of socks over her feet when he returned to her side.

"Time to go," he told her.

"What?" Shocked, she stared at him, trying to read more in his face. More what, she didn't know. All of a sudden, fear gripped her belly. This tent wasn't home. It wasn't even civilization. They were in the godforsaken middle of frozen hell. But this tent had become a haven. Safe and secure.

Now they had to leave?

He sat opposite her, tugging on his boots.

"They took Lukoski at 0400. The area is secure." He looked up from tying his laces to give her a quick smile. "You get to go home."

"Home." The image of her condo, with its bright colors and big soft bed, filled her head. Even better, the beach only five minutes away. Hot sand, warm water. She was going to spend her first two days home curled up under her blankets, sleeping like a baby. And the next handful on the beach soaking up as much sunshine as her body would hold.

"Can't go until you put your boots on, though," he prompted, handing them to her as if to hurry her along. She tugged, tied and stood in under a minute.

Not bad time for having spent part of it peering at her lover, trying to figure out why he felt so far away all of a sudden.

"Ready," she said as her head popped through the top of her sweater.

Busy with their outer gear, Blake didn't say anything.

"What about all this?" She gestured to the tent, the equipment. "Do we pack it up?"

He shook his head.

"A team will come in later, after we get you out of here."

"We should do the dishes." She looked at the cots, one pristine with blankets still tight enough to bounce a quarter on, the other mussed and tumbled, with two imprints clear on the pillow. "Or at least make the bed."

Blake followed her gaze with unreadable eyes. Why was he so distant now? Was he ashamed of what they'd done? Was he so tied to rules and regulations that he regretted their lovemaking? Or just that he'd opened up to her? Hadn't he meant what he said about wanting a full life? Or had he meant it, but realized that it simply didn't apply to her.

He handed her the heavy coat she'd worn on the trip in, then shrugged into his own. Before she could finish zipping hers closed, he tossed the can of chocolate into the trash bag, shook out the blankets and gave the pillow a good, solid punch.

Alexia winced. Her heart wept as she forced herself to finish securing the coat.

Good thing she hadn't bared her heart. It looked as though he was finished here.

13

BLAKE WANTED to punch something harder than a lousy pillow. A brick wall. A steel door. An angry lion. Anything.

Why then? Why did the call have to come then? Why not in an hour. Or two, even. That would have given him time to deal with the emotional mess he'd fallen into. To finish the discussion and bring, what had she called it before? Closure?

Yeah. *Closure.*

Because facts were facts. Feelings, no matter how intense and inviting, wouldn't change them. He wouldn't—couldn't—ask her to be a part of the life he'd chosen. No matter how much he loved her.

"Are you ready? The rescue team is meeting us at the top of the mountain in fifteen minutes."

"We have to climb a mountain?"

He wanted to laugh. He wished he could find a little humor in this ending. Some way to leave them both with smiles. But he couldn't.

"The rescue vehicle can't make it down to this elevation," he explained, his voice a little stiff. "It's not a big climb and there's a pulley system in place. It'll be like taking an escalator to the second floor of the mall."

"Just like the mall," she muttered, looking as irritated as he felt all of a sudden. "Except for the freezing temperatures, wind trying to knock us over and blinding snow. Maybe we could get a cinnamon bun when we get to the top."

Blake felt rotten. He knew she was reacting to his tone, to his attitude. Just because he knew they had no future didn't mean he wanted to make her angry. Or worse, upset.

There you go, Landon, he mocked. *Rescue a gal from a raving lunatic, have sex with her all night even though you know better, then make her feel lousy about it. The Stud of the Year trophy should arrive any day.*

"Cinnamon buns, hmm?" he said, trying for a light tone. He took a deep breath, then crossed over to finish securing her winter gear. "I'll see what I can do."

He made quick work of her gear. Within seconds, she was ready to brave the elements. Swathed like a mummy, her face concealed and her vivid hair under wraps, she was all eyes. That should mean she was less expressive. But those eyes spoke volumes. Worry, sadness, a regretful goodbye. They were all there, screaming at him loud and clear. So were the embers of passion, so easily ignited between them. All it'd take was a look in return. A word, not even a promise.

And he could keep this going.

She'd regret it, eventually.

She'd hate his job, his connection to a man she felt so negatively toward.

He'd hate hurting her, resent the silent—or eventually not-so-silent—pressure to change.

But between now and that happening, they could have a whole lot of time exploring that passion. Having incredible sex. Enjoying the hell out of each other.

That was living in the moment, wasn't it?

Even though you knew the moment was going to hurt like hell eventually.

"Let's rock and roll."

With that, and a quick smile, he pulled his own face gear into place and gestured her out the tent flap.

They didn't say another word, even when he hooked her safety line and showed her how to climb. It took them a solid ten minutes to traverse the ledge. When he'd arrived, after setting up the tent, he'd put the pulleys into place and carved hand- and footholds into the icy snow. They'd filled in a bit in the thirty or so hours since, making for a few dicey moments. But mostly it was a simple, easy extraction.

As before, Alexia kept up. He wanted to tell her she had military in her blood. She was as good, as solid, as many of the people he'd served with. But he didn't think she'd see that as a compliment.

At the top, he dug his fingers into the deep snow and heaved himself over the edge. Then he reached down for Alexia. Without hesitation, despite there being a thirty-foot drop behind her, she let go of the mountain and put her hand in his. He pulled her up, first over the edge, then to her feet.

They both looked around.

The sound came first. Like a purr beneath the roar of the wind, it slowly grew. Lights, blurred and hazy, bobbed toward them.

"Your chariot," he said, recognizing the light pattern, but still gesturing her behind a rock and pulling his gun. SOP until he saw the driver and knew it was safe.

"Boy Scout, this is Magic Carpet. Do you read?"

"This is Boy Scout, I read. You're in our sights."

"The package is ready to go?"

"Affirmative." The package was staring at him through

huge brown eyes as she listened to the communication through her own headset.

"Handoff is imminent. CHAOS will take delivery in person. Magic Carpet out."

Shit.

The admiral was in the Snow Trac?

He should warn Alexia. He might have wiggled out of personal responsibility for not telling her his connection to her father in the past, given the situation. But this time? He knew who her father was, where he was and, Blake eyed the lumbering vehicle still a mile away, just exactly when he'd arrive.

Telling her was against regulations.

Not telling her was the end of their chances together.

He pictured Phil's mom's face at the funeral. Someday, it could be him in the flag-covered box. Could he ask Alexia to accept that? To take the chance that someday she'd be sitting there, accepting a folded flag and military condolences?

Because he loved her enough to want forever, he realized with a painful grinding in his heart. And forever was something he couldn't promise.

Better to promise nothing, to ask nothing. And to make nothing available. She wouldn't get hurt that way.

And his hurt? The excruciating, gut-wrenching misery in his heart? Hey, he was a specially trained soldier, equipped to push through any pain and survive.

"Thank you," she said, her voice soft as a whisper through his headset.

Afraid of what else she'd say, Blake quickly shook his head, then pointed at the Snow Trac vehicle rumbling across the white expanse. Privacy time was over. Communications were open now. Wide-open.

Blake clenched his jaw.

Time to say goodbye.

ALEXIA WATCHED the huge monstrosity trudge toward them, looking like a giant metal turtle crossing the snow. It was her way home. Escape from the bizarre hell her life had turned into this last week.

So why did she have a desperate urge to shimmy back down the side of the mountain and hide in the tent?

Or better yet, burrow into Blake's arms and beg him not to let her go.

He hadn't let her thank him. Because they'd be overheard, or because he wasn't comfortable with the praise, she didn't know. But he'd saved her. Saved her life. Saved her virtue. And quite likely saved her sanity.

He was a hero. She watched him as he stood between her and the oncoming rescue vehicle, rifle at the ready. Even though he'd talked to them himself, he wouldn't take a chance with her safety until he was sure it was U.S. military in that snow-tank thing.

Everything he'd done suddenly crashed over her. All because he was a soldier. A SEAL. A hero. How could she take issue with that when it was because of all those things that she was alive? How could she ever wish him to do anything else when he was so fabulously talented at being a SEAL? As long as there were freaks and lunatics and evil in the world, men like Blake stood against them. Kept the rest of the world safe, just as he was keeping her safe now.

She wanted to thank him again. To tell him how much he meant to her, how much she appreciated what he did. And how wrong she'd been to reject him based on his job.

She wanted a chance.

A chance for them.

But now it was too late.

As if mocking the timing of her realization, the Snow Trac grumbled to a loud, whining stop twenty feet away.

The lights flashed. Code, she realized as Blake lowered his weapon.

"Your chariot," he told her, gesturing to the vehicle.

Everything she wanted to say was bottled up inside her like a shook-up soda. All intense and mixed up and ready to burst. She wanted to tell him so many things.

But she'd had her chance.

As she'd done so many times in the last day, she hooked her fingers in his belt and put her feet into the indentions he made in the snow.

They reached the vehicle and he gestured her to come around. Two soldiers stood on either side of the open door, both with rifles at the ready. Covering them, she realized with a nervous shiver.

"Be safe," Blake said as she moved toward the steps.

"What?" She turned back, shaking her head.

"Aren't you coming?" He had to be. She had so many things to say to him. So much to try to work out. "You're not staying here, are you?"

"I'm meeting my team back at the compound for cleanup," he said, sounding as official as if he'd been delivering a report to a superior. Or talking to a stranger.

Despite their audience, not caring how it was perceived, Alexia reached out one gloved hand. Before she could figure out what to say, how to say it, a familiar voice harrumphed.

"Well done, Landon. Now, move on to phase cleanup."

Ice formed along Alexia's spine. She felt like one wrong move and she'd crack into tiny pieces.

Suddenly as cold as she'd been in that tiny cell, she turned to face the man in the doorway of the Snow Trac. Like her and Blake and the rest of the soldiers, he was dressed in white camouflage, a helmet, mask and goggles obscuring his features. No matter, she'd know him anywhere.

"Father," she greeted quietly. "I didn't realize you were here."

"Let's go." That's all he said. No greeting. No explanation. Just an order.

Heart heavy, Alexia looked back at Blake. His lack of reaction told her that he wasn't surprised to see the admiral. He'd known he'd be there. And he hadn't warned her.

If he'd held up a sign that said Not Interested, the message couldn't have been clearer.

Shaking, her knees so wobbly that only pride allowed her to manage the steps into the vehicle, Alexia suddenly wanted to be gone. And she never, ever wanted to see snow again.

"Lieutenant," she said, looking over her shoulder to give Blake a nod to acknowledge all he'd done. Including breaking her heart. "Thank you."

"You sure you don't want some chocolate cake? Or maybe ice cream? I can run out and get fresh strawberries to go with it."

It took all her strength for Alexia to pull her gaze from the view of her parents' garden. The entire time she'd been doing her *hostage routine,* as her brother had termed it once he'd stopped crying, she'd fantasized about her own bed. Yet three days after she'd climbed into that Snow Trac and rolled out of hell, she still hadn't made it there.

At first, it was easier to stay here. Her father's connections and pull had meant the debriefing team and the navy psychologist made house calls. The admiral's gruff attitude had meant that Edward, filled with guilt that she'd been kidnapped for research he'd instigated, kept his exhausting visits to a minimum. And her mother's newly found nurturing streak—and her chef—had meant that Alexia was pampered beyond belief. Margaret had even called in her beauty team and a masseuse that morning to give her daughter some much-needed pampering.

"I'm okay," she told her worried-looking mother. She'd never realized Margaret had the hovering gene, but for the last couple of days it'd been out in megaforce. "I'm still full from lunch."

"Lunch was four hours ago. You're not eating enough."

"I was only gone five days, Mother. Not nearly enough time to lose weight and need constant feeding," Alexia said with a teasing look. She patted the belly of her jeans to show it still wasn't flat.

Her smile faded as her mother's face crumpled. And not, Alexia knew, because she was horrified at her daughter's curves.

"Don't," she begged, sliding from the bench seat and wrapping her arms around her mother. "Please. You keep crying and I'm going to need a transfusion. You know I'm a sympathy weeper."

"I was scared," Margaret admitted. "I've never been scared like that before." Her fingers clutched her daughter for just a second before she sniffed, stepped back and carefully dabbed the dampness from under her eyes.

Alexia dropped back to the window seat and stared in shock.

"You were scared?" But she'd seemed so calm when she'd welcomed Alexia home. Margaret had gotten a little weird, with the hovering and all. But Alexia hadn't realized that was fear.

"What do you think?" Margaret snapped. "My daughter, kidnapped by a lunatic. Hauled off to some icy hellhole. We didn't know who, or why. And when we did, it was even worse."

She paused to take a deep breath, then continued. "I was terrified. Your father was, too, although he tried not to show it. He called in every marker he had, Alexia. He handpicked the SEAL team, he demanded the best to rescue you. Even then, we had no idea…"

Her words trailed off, and she sniffed, but held her hand out to say she was getting control of herself. So Alexia stayed seated. Truthfully, she was too surprised at the idea of her father worrying to have the strength to stand.

"Michael and I waited here, of course. But your father refused to. He insisted on going to Alaska to get you. He even yelled at Daniel Lane."

"He yelled at the rear admiral?"

Reeling a little and not sure how to deal with it, Alexia absently patted the cushion next to her. To her surprise, her mother took the invitation and sat.

"As I said," Margaret told her with a quick, uncomfortable pat to the knee, "I've never been so scared."

"You must have been, though. I mean, Father served his entire career in the military. He fought in two wars. How was that not scary?"

Heck, just thinking of Blake doing cleanup at that nasty compound gave her chest palpitations.

"Because that was his job," Margaret said with a flick of her bejeweled wrist, as if dismissing the question as ridiculous. Alexia waited to feel slighted, stupid, as she would have so often in the past when her curiosity was rebuffed. But her mother didn't seem to be closing the dialogue. Just responding.

"It's that easy? Because it's his job, you weren't afraid?"

"Darling, he was trained to fight. Trained in strategy. He knew how to use weapons and all of that big scary equipment and had an entire platoon of men just as well trained, just as dedicated, fighting at his side. As I said, it was his job. And he was very, very good at it."

"But his job put him in constant danger. He had people shooting at him, trying to blow him up. Didn't that worry you?"

"Did you watch the news yesterday?" Margaret asked.

Shaking her head no, Alexia frowned. What did that have to do with anything?

"I don't recall what city it was—I just caught the tail end of the newscast. But it was rush-hour traffic and someone became angry. He stopped his car in the middle of grid-locked traffic, pulled out a weapon and started shooting. He killed three people before he was stopped."

Alexia's breath caught at the horror. "Those poor people," she breathed.

"Exactly. They were only trying to get home, living their safe day-to-day lives. And someone tried to kill them." A combination of anger, disgust and pity creased Margaret's face. "At least a solider is trained and prepared. Nobody knows when their time is going to come, darling. It could be on a mission, or at the grocery store. So sitting around wringing one's hands and worrying is a waste of time and energy, don't you think?"

She nodded, and the little ball of terror that'd knotted in her belly when she realized she was in love with Blake started to unravel. But right next to it was a bigger fear, one that was still tied tight.

Taking a deep breath, she asked, "But what about the rest? The fact that most of his life is dedicated to the service. That he keeps tons of secrets from you. How does that not bother you?"

Her mother looked stunned for a second, as if she'd never considered those questions. Then she shrugged.

"Well, that too is a part of his job, isn't it? I knew it

when I married him, so why would it bother me? As for the secrets…" She glanced at the door, then laughed and lifted both hands as if to say *well?* "Darling, I have plenty of secrets of my own. Secrets that your father will never find out about."

Alexia's eyes rounded with shock.

"Noooo?" she breathed.

"Mine might not be along the lines of military intelligence, but they're juicy enough. Like the true color of my hair, for instance. Or my real weight and collection of Spanx. Your father thinks I eat half a grapefruit every morning, but has no idea I have a bowl of Cocoa Puffs after he leaves for the day." Margaret tapped one manicured finger on her lips as she considered what else she might be hiding from her husband. "There are the two credit cards he doesn't know I have. For my girlie purchases, of course. He has no idea that I love trash-talk television in the daytime, or that when he's out of town I eat chocolate in bed."

"And you keep all this from him?" Alexia felt stunned, not so much that her mother kept secrets, but that she had such fun ones to hide.

"Of course. It's all a part of my job of being happy while presenting the ladylike image that's so important to supporting your father's career. And don't you forget, this information is classified, young lady, and disseminated only on a need-to-know basis."

Alexia laughed until tears trickled down her cheeks. Her mother, watching with a bright smile, reached over to tuck a curl behind her ear, letting her fingers smooth her daughter's cheek as she did.

Smiling, Alexia was pretty sure this was the closest, the happiest, she'd ever been with her mother.

"Why didn't you ever share any of this with me before?" she asked.

"You never wanted to hear it before, darling. You were too busy rebelling and finding your own way." Margaret patted her daughter's knee, then rose. "And you do have a habit of holding on to anger, Alexia. Long after a battle has ended, you're still there in the trenches, ready to aim and fire again. Which makes communication rather difficult."

Well, there you go. Alexia's shoulders sank under the weight of that truth. Her parents weren't perfect. Nor was she so overwhelmed by the emotions of her ordeal into thinking they were even great. They were self-absorbed, stubborn, close-minded and ambitious.

But, she realized, so was she.

"Mother, is it okay if I stay here again tonight?"

"I'd love it if you did," Margaret said. Then her smile dimmed a little. "But we do have company coming for dinner. You're free to join us, or if you're still feeling melancholy, you can take your meal in your room."

"I'll join you," Alexia decided, surprising them both. Hey, maybe a meal where she wasn't *holding on to anger* would be interesting.

"I'll let the cook know," Margaret said, her eyes bright again.

She left with a quick wave of her fingers. Alexia heard her in the hallway, then her father's deeper tones. He was home from the base. Other than his insistence on being there for the debriefing—which she'd thought was to make sure she didn't embarrass him but now wondered if it was for support—she hadn't seen him since their return from the North Slope. And even that she didn't remember much of. After ten silent, miserable minutes in the Snow Trac trying not to cry, she'd fallen asleep only to wake on an aircraft carrier just before it set down in Coronado.

Should she go talk with him?

Try to discover if there might be a bridge between them like the one she'd found with her mother?

Ask if he had news of Blake and whether or not the team was back yet?

Double-check to see if she'd drooled all over the cot in his aircraft carrier?

She should.

If she wanted an open dialogue and communication between them, it was up to her to take the first step.

And maybe her mother had a point. Maybe she did hold on to anger, creating walls where there didn't need to be any.

Then again, what if all he wanted to do was lecture her? Or chide her on her career choices? Or any number of other negative things.

Things had always been cut-and-dried between them— her father was the jerk, she was the poor, misunderstood and unappreciated daughter. He was rigid, she was strong. He was wrong, she was right. Simple as that.

Now she didn't know. Wasn't sure.

"Who's in the mood for cinnamon buns?"

Saved from talking herself into approaching her father, Alexia gratefully looked up to see her brother standing in the doorway, a white, aromatic bag in hand.

"Michael," she greeted, rising to give him a tight hug. "Are you here again? I thought you had a show today."

"Show, shmow. I took a little personal time. It's not every year that my sister scares the crap out of me, after all."

"That seems to be today's theme," Alexia said, taking the bag even though she wasn't hungry. At this rate, she'd be ten pounds overweight before she ever made it home.

"Are you okay?" Michael asked, pulling a chair over

and straddling it. "What scared you? Flashbacks? Nightmares? Split ends?"

Alexia's lips quirked. She pulled a piece off the bun, but didn't eat it. "Mother said she was scared. When I was gone, she said you all were. I mean, I knew *you* would be. But I didn't even consider that they would."

"She was pretty freaked," Michael said. "And yeah, I'd have to say Father was, too. He cussed up a storm, threw a few things and ordered me to stay here and take care of Mom while he dealt with this mess."

Alexia's lips twitched. "This mess?"

"Yeah. But he didn't mean you for once," Michael teased with a wink. "He was talking about the Science Institute. Dr. Darling was being a total ass about the rescue, wanting to do some CYA before bringing in the authorities. He didn't want the news leaking before he'd talked to the investors."

CYA. Covering his ass, indeed.

"That Edward sure is a peach," she said sardonically. She wasn't surprised, though. He'd been in contact with the terrorist for almost a year and hadn't caught on that the guy was a murdering lunatic. If that got out, he wasn't going to look so good. And bad press could slam the door shut on the flow of money to the institute. But still, the man had claimed they were perfect for each other. Maybe he'd have been in a bigger rush to rescue her if she'd slept with him.

As if reading her mind, Michael nudged her shoulder with his. "Good thing you didn't date the guy, hmm? I mean, what a wank."

She made a sound of agreement, staring out the window again. She'd thought Edward's only drawback was that he didn't turn her on. But it looked as if all the communication skills in the world didn't make a guy a hero.

"Are you staying for dinner?" she asked.

"Are you?"

"Sure. Mother said there would be guests. But you can sit next to me and keep me entertained."

And distracted. Because all this self-reflection was really messing with her resolve to accept that things were over with Blake.

Of course, resolve or not, it didn't really matter.

He was the one who wanted nothing to do with her.

14

BLAKE STOOD AT ATTENTION, waiting for the admiral's signal.

"At ease," Pierce said as he moved behind the imposing desk in his home office and sat like a king on his leather throne. "You're a guest, Landon, relax and have a seat."

Right.

Blake sat, but he didn't relax. The venue was a little more informal than headquarters, where he'd had his first debriefing. And he might be the admiral's dinner guest, but that didn't change the fact that this was a formal interview.

"You've already received official acknowledgment of a job well done," the admiral said, his fingers steepled in front of his chest as he regarded Blake. The look on his face might have been friendly, but it was hard to tell. Granite didn't bend well. "I'd like to offer my private, personal appreciation, as well. You got my daughter out, kept her safe and delivered her without harm. Her mother and I are grateful."

Blake stared. For real? He hadn't taken the admiral as a gratitude kind of guy.

"Thank you, sir," he said. Then, knowing he shouldn't, he still asked, "How is Alexia doing? Has she recovered from her ordeal?"

Meaning the "kidnapping and grueling weather" ordeal. Not the "sex on a cot and subsequent pseudo rejection from him" ordeal. Blake ground his teeth, still not sure if he'd done the right thing. Or more to the point, still not sure he was glad he'd done the right thing.

He missed her. He'd spent eight months missing her, but telling himself she hated him had made it easier to resist the urge to reconnect. Now that he knew she didn't hate him…? The urge was like a noxious rash, growing and spreading at lightning speed, making him crazy.

"According to the psychologist, she's processed the trauma in a healthy way and isn't likely to have long-term issues as a result." Before Blake could process how stupid that sounded, the admiral continued, "According to her mother, she's fragile and underfed, but just needs some time and TLC. And if you listen to her brother, who knows her best, she's stewing over something and needs to go shoe shopping."

"Shoe shopping?" Blake deadpanned.

"Apparently it's a cure-all," the older man said, looking both baffled and embarrassed. Then he pulled his official face back on. "The bottom line is she's fine. A great deal of the credit for that goes to you."

"I'd say the credit for that goes directly to Alexia," Blake shot back without thinking.

And immediately regretted it. The admiral got a wily, weighing sort of look in his eyes. Then he nodded as if Blake had just made some grand confession.

"I'm going to step outside of protocol for a moment," Pierce said, folding his hands on his desk. He leaned forward, his face creasing in a granitelike smile. "I'd like to talk to you, not as your commanding officer, but man-to-man."

Blake's brows arched. Technically, since he was retired,

the admiral wasn't still his commanding officer. *Technically.* Still, it was the man-to-man part that was worrying.

"You and my daughter have…"

Oh, shit. Have what? Had inappropriate relations? Had a hundred or so mutual orgasms? Had enough emotional intensity between them to fuel a soap opera?

"You have a lot in common. You're both young and single."

Blake waited. Was that all Pierce had? Or did he simply not know enough about his daughter to make a list. Blake could. They liked the same music and laughed at the same jokes. They both liked the beach and hated being cold. They were communications specialists who specialized in avoiding communication. They had a sexual chemistry that could blow up both their worlds, and a mutual love for chocolate.

"You're both intense, focused individuals with strong ethics and career goals," the admiral finally said, a hint of triumph in his tone. Yep, the old guy really knew what young single people were looking for in each other.

"Sir, are you trying to set me up with Alexia?"

After she'd reacted so well to it the last time?

"*Set up* is such a juvenile term. Let's just say I'd be amenable to the idea of you and my daughter building a relationship together."

In all his consideration of whether a relationship with Alexia was a good idea or not, in all his continual recounting of the pros and cons, he'd never, once, factored her father's approval into the mix.

Now that it was front and center, he still didn't care. If he and Alexia were going to try to work things out, it'd be between the two of them. It didn't matter to him whether the admiral was cheering them on, or doing his damndest to roadblock them.

But they weren't going to try, because there was no point. A relationship between them would eventually hurt Alexia. Blake figured it was better to hurt her a little now, instead of a whole lot later.

"I'm sorry, sir. But I'm not in the market for a relationship. Besides," Blake couldn't resist adding, "I have a dangerous career. The chances of my being hurt, or killed, aren't insignificant. That's a lot to ask someone to live with."

That the admiral waved his concern away didn't surprise Blake. But his next words did. "She grew up with the realities of a soldier's life. She knows danger is relative. There are plenty of other dangerous careers. Police work, firefighting. Hell, my daughter just proved it's not even safe to work in a science laboratory. She's not going to worry about how safe your job is."

He wanted to believe that. He wished like crazy that he wouldn't be condemning her to a life of misery if he pursued this heat between them. But the image of Phil's mother's face wouldn't fade from his mind.

"I'd worry, sir. You know as well as I do that our work requires total focus. How can you give it that focus if a part of you…" Blake winced, realizing he was treading dangerously close to sappy greeting-card territory here. But he still wanted the answer. "How do you do your job right if your thoughts are back home, worrying about the people who are worrying about you?"

"You do it because they expect you to. Because they believe you're damn good and trust your training is the best." The admiral shrugged, then poked a beefy finger at the framed photo of his wife sitting on the corner of his desk. "You make sure they understand your reasons for being a soldier, that they are strong enough to support you. And you let them blubber when they have to. Give them some pats on the back, a little reassurance and make sure they know how you feel. Then, if something does happen, they're ready. They know why you did what you did and they know your feelings for them. With that, once the shock is over, they can accept it."

Well. Nonplussed, Blake stared. Talk about sappy greeting-card fodder.

But sappy or not, maybe the admiral was right. Blake had taken the loss of Phil hard, but he'd never questioned continuing to be a SEAL. He'd never questioned Phil's dedication to his job. Nor, he recalled, had Phil's mom.

"The only concern your career would have to my daughter is the secrecy. She's a stickler for talking. Communicating and all that rot." The admiral shook his head as if the idea of a couple communicating with each other was bizarre.

It was as if someone had just flicked on a bright light straight into his brain, and Blake blinked with surprise. Not only at the totally accurate insight, but that Pierce actually knew his daughter well enough to make it.

Still… He couldn't—wouldn't—change who he was. So secrecy was just as valid a reason as danger to avoid getting hurt… No, he corrected, to avoid hurting Alexia.

"I appreciate you considering me suitable for your daughter," Blake said, doing a careful verbal tap dance. "But, again, my career is my priority right now. I don't feel there's room for a relationship. Sir."

He tacked that last word on because the old guy's face looked as if it was going to crack.

Instead, it was the man's fist against his desk that snapped.

"She needs someone strong. Someone who will guide her, keep her out of trouble."

"She's strong enough to guide herself," Blake pointed

out, starting to get a little irked. "And the only trouble she's been in was through no fault of her own. I hardly think that calls for parental interference."

Blake tossed the words out like a grenade. With a lot of caution, full awareness that they were going to cause an explosion and a mental warning to be ready to duck and cover.

"You don't think being held in a terrorist cell, by a man convicted of five murders to date, is call for parental concern?" The admiral's expression was neutral, but his tone could cut ice. Both fists on his desk, he leaned forward with a lethal glare. "She won't listen to her mother or I, so she needs someone there. Someone who will protect her. Who will caution her and guide her into making more intelligent choices. To quit this ridiculous job and do something else. Private practice, counseling. If she'd done that before, perhaps she wouldn't be fragile, underfed and needing to buy shoes right now."

Blake wasn't sure how anyone could question Alexia's intelligence. But he figured he'd give Pierce the benefit of the doubt and call this fatherly concern. Or something.

"She doesn't want to do counseling," Blake said with a frown. "She wants to do research, to help people on a larger scale."

"She has two degrees. There's absolutely no reason for her to be involved in such a crackpot field except as an embarrassment to her family."

"She's researching subliminal sexual healing because she believes in it," Blake said slowly. A man of few illusions, he was still surprised that the admiral would go so far as trying to set his daughter up in a relationship in order to control her career choices.

"She could believe in something else just as easily," the older man said.

"She believes she's making a difference in the world."

"She's going on television and talking to reporters about sex."

"She's trying to help people who've been abused and have no other options. That means keeping the topic, and the funding, fresh and relevant. Yes, she's talking sex. But she does it with charm, humor and compassion."

If Blake tried, he was pretty sure he could hear the admiral's teeth grinding together.

"I could find a way to make this an order, Landon."

"Your daughter isn't under your command. Sir." Bitterness coating his mouth, Blake bit off the title. For the first time since he'd joined the service at eighteen, he actually wished he could spit on it.

"But *you* are. And you have influence with her."

Since the admiral still served on base as a civilian adviser, Blake had to give him that point.

"I don't have, nor would I use, influence to coerce someone into leaving a job they love. I would resent someone doing that to me, and would expect the same resentment in return."

Clearly, that wasn't what Pierce wanted to hear. His face closed tight, the admiral steepled his fingers, then launched his pièce de résistance. "I've still got pull on the base. You'd be smart to follow my orders."

The threat hung between them.

And it was a doozy. With the right word in the wrong ear, Blake could be off the SEAL team. He could be dumped in a training camp somewhere, teaching BUDS to swim. He could be doing push-ups in Guam.

The admiral had that kind of power.

Blake didn't give a damn.

Ready to refuse, he took a deep breath and rose to his

feet. Before he could say a word, there was a soft tap at the door.

He and the admiral both turned.

It was Alexia. Blake almost dropped back to his seat. Damn, she was gorgeous.

"Gentlemen," she greeted softly. The look she gave Blake was guarded. Impossible to read.

"Yes?" her father barked.

"Mother asked me to let you know dinner is ready," Alexia said quietly, addressing her words to her father but not taking her gaze off Blake.

"Very well." The admiral's chair squeaked as he rose. "We'll continue this discussion after the meal, Landon."

"I think we've finished it already, sir."

He should care that he'd just put his career on the line. It should matter that he was risking everything, his job, his identity, his world, in refusing the admiral's request that he manipulate Alexia.

But all Blake could see, focus on, was her. Standing in the doorway, she looked like sunset.

Her curls tumbled, soft and flowing, over bare shoulders. Unlike the last time they'd been together, when the only color on her face was the bruises under her eyes and her cold-chapped cheeks, she was fully made-up. Like a siren, her eyes were deep and mysterious, her lips red and luscious. She wore a sundress of bleeding turquoise and purple, the silky fabric hugging her curves, then flaring from the hips to swing, full and frothy, to her knees. It was an old-fashioned look, like something a fifties pinup would wear. It suited her perfectly.

She was gorgeous.

He wanted to reach out and touch her. To see if she felt as good as she looked.

"Ahem."

Blake's gaze shot to the admiral. The older man stood in the doorway glowering. Not nearly as encouraging a look as the old man had offered when he'd been hoping to hook his daughter up with Blake. Then again, he'd clearly thought Blake a lot more malleable then.

"If you don't mind, Father," Alexia said, finally pulling her gaze from Blake's to give the admiral a small smile, "I'd appreciate a few moments alone. I wasn't able to thank Lieutenant Landon adequately before. I'd like to now."

"Dinner is waiting."

Blake wondered if his invitation to dine was still good. The other man didn't say otherwise, though, so he figured it was.

"It'll just be a few moments," Alexia said. Then, in a move that shocked all three of them, she laid her hand on her father's arm. "Please."

For a second, the admiral looked as if she'd pulled a gun on him. Then he gave a gruff nod, awkwardly patted her hand and turned to go. He even pulled the door shut behind him.

"Holy shit," Blake said, almost whispering. "How'd you do that?"

"I'm really not sure," she told him with a little laugh, giving the closed door a wide-eyed look. "But enjoy it while you can, since he'll probably be back soon."

Blake's grin only lasted a second, then faded as he stared at her. Damn, she looked good. Now that they were alone, he wanted to grab her and hold tight. To haul her off to the nearest private space that didn't have her father's stamp on it, and have his wild way with her.

He wanted to get the hell out before he gave in to any of those things and hurt them both.

"We should join them," Blake said, gesturing to the door and wherever beyond it the dining room was.

"In just a second." Looking at her feet, shod in impressively high fuchsia pumps, Alexia chewed on her lip, then gave a sigh and met his eyes. "I really do want to thank you. I also wanted to apologize. And, as soon as I confess, I'll have to do both of those again, but I should get the first one out of the way, well, first," she babbled.

Blake stared at her, trying to unravel her words.

Despite the gravity of her tone, her eyes danced as she watched him try to work it out.

"What do you want to thank me for?" he asked, starting at the top.

"For rescuing me." She held up one hand as if to halt his objection. "Yes, I know I thanked you already and you will claim it was just your job. But this is for more than rescuing me."

"You want to thank me for holding your hand?" he asked, trying to make a joke out of what was surely going to be an emotional mess.

"Well, you are pretty amazing at the hand-holding," she teased. Her voice was low and sexy, bringing back all kinds of memories of her naked body, his exploding climax, the sounds she made as she took her pleasure.

God, he wanted her. And not just sex with her. He wanted that about as much as he wanted his next breath, but thinking about it in the admiral's office gave him visions of the brig.

"But I wanted to thank you for a little more than that," she said, pulling him off the ride to fantasyland. "I was scared. Even after you got me out of that nightmare, I was scared. You kept me from falling apart. You made me feel safe."

"That's my job," he dismissed, trying to shrug the discomfort off his shoulders.

"Yes, that's the point. It is your job. Your job, what you

do, makes people feel safe." She stepped forward, close enough that the familiar, heady scent of her shampoo enveloped him in a subtle cloud. "I threw your career in your face last year. I used it and, well, your connection to my father as an excuse to slam the door shut between us."

Since Blake had done exactly that himself, he'd have to be a pretty big ass to hold a grudge. Or even to pretend to, for the sake of keeping a wedge between them. "You have every reason to see my career as an issue," he told her. "It is one. I'm not a good relationship bet. I'm not going to be around a lot of weekends to go out. I'm not a 'home at five for dinner' kind of guy. I live on the edge and that takes a toll."

He shoved his hands into the front pockets of his slacks and resisted the urge to kick the thick leg of the admiral's desk. That was all true. That, and so much more. But he wanted, insanely and with all his heart, to ask her to take a chance anyway. To let him love her, despite those challenges.

But he couldn't. He loved her too much to ask that of her.

"My career is who I am," he said with a resigned shrug. "Relationship success with guys like me is pretty hard to come by. So rejecting me last year? That was a smart move."

"You think I was right to reject you?"

His wince was minuscule, more an ego reflex than regret.

"I think we have too many things stacked against us. My career, your upbringing. Your father, my…" His voice trailed off. Even in the name of full honesty, he couldn't bring himself to admit that he was still grieving. Instead, he shrugged as though his heart wasn't weeping like a sad, little baby. "Like you said last year, the issues between us are too big."

ALEXIA FOLDED HER FINGERS together, then flexed them apart before twining them together again. He listed all the same reasons they shouldn't be together that she'd already told herself.

She should be grateful. And to show that gratitude, she should finish her thank-yous and let the man have his dinner.

"You're right," she told him. "Your career is a big part of who you are. Just as mine is a big part of who I am."

She saw it, the flicker of anger in his eyes. It was that fury on her behalf that did it. That tipped the scales over from smart to heart.

"Which brings me to the confession, apology and second thank-you," she said, surreptitiously stepping closer. Close enough to breathe in his scent. To feel his warmth. To see deep into his eyes and revel in the heat there.

"You might want to make it fast. I doubt your father's going to wait long before reminding us we're missing the meal," he said, looking toward the door then back, shifting from one foot to the other. Was he nervous? How sweet was that, Alexia thought, almost smiling.

"Actually, my mother knows I wanted to speak with you. She'll keep Father from interrupting." Yet another shock to add to the many of the day. All it'd taken was a request and the word *please* and her mother had been happy to run interference.

"Okay. Confession?" he prompted, shifting away a few inches.

This time she did smile. She liked that she made the big bad SEAL worry. It gave her hope for the rest of this discussion.

"I listened at the door," she told him softly. Then, using his shock, she stepped right into his space and looked up at him with wide-eyed innocence. "I heard my name and couldn't help myself."

"Your father doesn't like your job," was all he said. He didn't rat out the admiral's threats. He didn't claim hero-ship for standing up for her. This was it, she realized. Her chance to use that angry-grudge habit her mother had commented on and turn it into Blake keeping secrets from her.

Except she knew better.

"My father is commanding, overbearing and arrogant," she said with a shrug. "But he's also right."

"That you should leave your job?" That shocked him and caused just a little anger, if his frown was anything to go by. "Why? Because he's got a puritanical streak? Or because some asshole terrorized you and tried to use you to create a weapon?"

"Why does it sound like you'd be equally angry if I answered yes to either of those?" she mused.

"I think its bullshit that you let anyone bully you. For any reason."

Alexia nodded. "I agree. Nobody has the right, even in the name of love, to try to control someone else's life."

Blake frowned. "Even if you think you're doing it to keep them safe? Or because you believe a relationship can't exist on half-truths?"

"You know, there are elements of my job that are classified. That I'm not supposed to discuss," she told him, twining her fingers with his. He didn't pull away, but she could feel the tension in him, as if he wanted to run. Or grab her. She figured if she held on long enough to stop him from doing the former, he'd go for the latter. "Would you have an issue with that? I mean, my job revolves around sexuality. I'm constantly dealing with people's sexual fantasies, figuring out what turns them on. I'm a scientist. We do a lot in the name of experimentation."

She left it there, with all that innuendo hanging out exposed and ugly.

He frowned, as if he'd never thought of her job in those terms before. Then he gave her a *nice-try* look.

"So you'd be okay with a relationship filled with secrets? One that didn't have total openness and honesty?" he asked, his tone calling bullshit on that.

"No."

He nodded, as if he knew he was right.

"I need total openness and honesty in a relationship," she said slowly. "Or I should say emotional openness and honesty."

"I can't stop what I do, Alexia." He lifted both her hands to his lips and brushed her knuckles with soft kisses. Then, sounding as if he was ripping the words from his gut, he added, "Not even for you. And what I do is dangerous. I lost one of my best friends last year. He caught a piece of shrapnel right in front of me. I know how it feels to have to go on after that. I've seen how hard it is on the people left behind. I've lived it. I can't ask someone to do that for me."

"You see," she said, inching just a little closer so the wide hem of her dress brushed his legs. "That's emotionally open and honest. That's what's important. Not the details of a mission or the location of your next raid."

Frowning, he shook his head.

"I don't think you heard me."

"I did," she promised. "I heard every word. But I responded to what really mattered. I'm okay with the danger. That's what my father was right about. I grew up surrounded by hundreds, thousands of men who lived with that danger. And most of those men are still around. You are specially trained to deal with that part of your job. That doesn't mean training eliminates the danger, or that horrible things won't still happen. But they happen anyway."

"Like your kidnapping," he said quietly.

"Exactly." *Thank you, Father,* she mentally sang, grateful that the admiral had laid the groundwork for that argument. "But the secrets, the danger? If we can communicate, if we're emotionally honest, then we can work through any issues those things create."

He didn't look as distant and closed now, but his blue eyes were still cautious. Watchful. As though he knew there was a flaw in her argument, but he just hadn't found it yet.

Because he was so worried about a trap, Alexia stepped away. Put some distance between them. Just because she'd reached a place where she felt good about pursuing this relationship, where she'd justified it all in her mind, that didn't mean he had. Or that he would.

Fear clutched at her belly. Her breath tight, she tried to remind herself that she'd faced death, dammit. This chasing down the man she loved? Piece of cake.

She pressed her hand against her churning stomach. Okay, so maybe more like an entire decadently rich, double-fudge-chocolate cake eaten in its entirety in a single sitting. In other words, she felt like puking. But it'd be worth it, she promised herself.

"I have a relationship with your father," Blake said as if he were laying another card on the table, slowly showing his hand one point at a time. "He's no longer active on base, but he was my mentor for years. He'll continue to have input into my career."

Then he grimaced and added, "Unless he follows through on those threats, of course. Then I'll probably be stationed on Guam."

"Ironically, I'm starting to think I might have a relationship with my father, too," she said, still not sure how she felt about that. "I doubt it'll ever be a close one, or even cordial. But I'm beginning to believe that maybe it doesn't have to be antagonistic and angry any longer."

"Wow," he breathed.

"I know," she said with a laugh. "Look at me, all grown up."

His gaze skimmed her body, as if reminding them both of just how grown up she was. Her blood heated, her breath slowed. She wanted him like crazy, and dammit, they had to get through this issue and then dinner with her parents before she could have him. So they'd better hurry up or she wouldn't be able to resist giving him a toe massage during the dessert course.

"If your job wasn't an issue, if the danger and secrets didn't exist, would you want to be in a relationship with me?" she asked, putting it all on the table. The questions, the opening, her heart. All there for him to take or leave.

"They are an issue."

"If they weren't," she insisted, giving him a *quit-being-stubborn* look.

"If they weren't an issue," he said slowly, so slowly she wanted to scream at him to quit tormenting her, "I'd be begging you to go out with me. I'd be doing my damnedest to sweep you off your feet. I'd have you in bed so fast, the sheets would catch fire."

Relief, pleasure and excitement poured through Alexia, making her want to grab him close for a hug, then dance around the room laughing.

"Then why are you making them an issue? I've made my peace with them, so now it's up to you. It's not because of me that these things stand between us." There it was, the truth gauntlet. Tossed between them in challenge. Now it was all up to him.

"I watched what it did to Phil's family, saying goodbye to him," he said quietly, his eyes boring into hers with an intensity that made her want to cry. "I saw the devastation. How could you ask me to do that to you?"

"There are no guarantees, Blake. All you can do is make every day we have together one that I could treasure, in case something did happen. Isn't that all anyone can do?"

He frowned, looking as if he was turning her words over and over in his mind. Trying to find the flaw, to figure out how to dismiss them.

Alexia wanted to tell him to get over it already. To agree they had a chance. She wanted to run from the room and hide, so she didn't have to face rejection. And mostly, she wanted to grab back the last eight months, to go back to the time that he'd believed they had a chance. Before her fears had fueled his, before she'd given him enough reason to believe that she wasn't strong enough to handle a future with him.

But she couldn't. Instead, she had to accept that she'd given it her best. With all his issues on the table, she'd answered each the best she could.

Well, she did have one argument left. But it made her feel naked. Terrified. And, again, a little like throwing up.

Faced with probable rejection, she couldn't do it. She couldn't tell him she loved him, only to be turned away.

"Here's the thing. I can't date you," he finally said, his words low, quiet. As if the words were torn from him.

It took all her willpower to keep her smile in place and not look as if she'd just been kicked in the gut. But Alexia did it. Hey, something to be proud of.

"Well, then…" She took a breath, still smiling, dammit, and looked around. "I guess we should go in and join the dinner party. I'm sure our presence will help my father's digestion."

And the sooner she took him into the dining room, the sooner she could get a sudden migraine and have to go lie down. Looking forward to that, Alexia turned toward the door.

She didn't make a single step before Blake grabbed her hands and drew her back.

Gasping, she started to pull away. Then realized she was exactly where she wanted to be and stopped, sliding closer to him with a challenging look instead.

"Yes?" she asked in a long, slow drawl.

"Here's the thing," he said, sliding his fingers into hers and pulling her close so both hands were captured in his behind the small of her back. "I can't date you, because that's not enough."

"You want sex, too?" she teased, shifting just a little closer so her hips brushed his.

"Hell, yeah," he responded, grinning. Then he shook his head and gave her a chiding look. "But that's not where I was going."

"I thought that's always where you wanted to go." She was having trouble containing the giddiness she felt. Crazy, since she wasn't even sure what she was giddy about. But she needed the answer to what was standing between them as much as he needed to say it, so she bit her lip and said, "Sorry. Why can't you date me?"

"We've got stuff between us, things that can be problems. I know your father will interfere. I know my career, your temper, they'll be challenging. But the things that matter, they're stronger."

"My temper?" she asked, giving him a wide-eyed look. Then her brow twitched. Hadn't her mother mentioned that very issue earlier? Clearly she had some self-reflection to do. Especially if it might fix the problem between her and Blake. "What are the things that do matter to you, then?"

He gave her a look so intense, her stomach plummeted to her toes and hid.

"I want a future. A commitment. A chance to see if this thing between us—the explosive heat and sweet humor and weird wavelength connection—to see if those are real. If they last."

A future? This time when Alexia bit her lip, it was to keep herself from crying with joy.

"They've lasted over eight months," she said, smiling so big her face actually hurt.

"I want to see if they last day in and day out. If we can both do our jobs, live together and still do that emotional honesty thing that's so important to you."

"Do you think we can?" she asked, willing to put one thousand percent in but needing to know he was just as committed.

"I think I love you enough to make sure we do," he said quietly. So quietly that it took a second for his words to sink in. Alexia's eyes rounded. Her heart jumped. The only reason she didn't throw her arms around his neck and squeal was that he had her hands still clasped behind her back.

"You love me?" she repeated quietly. "Me, with the temper and the sex job and the nightmare of a father? Me who insists on talking through all these emotional things and will always be asking you how you feel?"

"You, who are sweet and sexy, smart and funny. You who keep me from hiding inside myself," he said quietly, resting his forehead on hers. "You who make me feel like a hero, and keep me on my toes."

"Yep," she decided with a giggle as she pressed tiny kisses over his face. "That's me. The same me that loves you right back."

Blake's eyes closed, as if in thanks. Then he took her mouth in a kiss filled with as much passion as it was promises. With as much hope as there was heat.

"What d'ya say we skip dinner?" he said against her lips.

"Sneak around the back?" she suggested, tilting her head toward the glass door leading to the side yard. "My father will have a fit."

"I live for danger, remember." Grinning, he slid his arms under her and swept her off her feet.

Still holding her close, he nudged open the French doors and carried her through.

Alexia held on tight, her head snuggled against his chest.

"My hero," she whispered.

* * * * *